D0832425

LEVELS TO THIS SHYT

Ah'Million

Lock Down Publications and Ca$h
Presents
Levels to This Shyt
A Novel by *Ah'Million*

Ah'Million

Lock Down Publications
P.O. Box 944
Stockbridge, Ga 30281
www.lockdownpublications.com

Copyright 2021 by Ah'Million
Levels to This Shyt

All rights reserved. No part of this book may be reproduced in any form or by electronic or mechanical means, including information storage and retrieval systems without permission in writing from the publisher, except by a reviewer who may quote brief passages in review.
First Edition January 2021
Printed in the United States of America

This is a work of fiction. Names, characters, places, and incidents either are products of the author's imagination or are used fictitiously. Any similarity to actual events or locales or persons, living or dead, is entirely coincidental.

Lock Down Publications
Like our page on Facebook: Lock Down Publications @
www.facebook.com/lockdownpublications.ldp
Cover design and layout by: **Dynasty Cover Me**
Book interior design by: **Shawn Walker**
Edited by: **Jill Alicea**

4

Stay Connected with Us!

Text **LOCKDOWN** to 22828 to stay up-to-date with
new releases, sneak peaks, contests and more...
Or CLICK HERE to sign up.

Thank you!

Like our page on Facebook:

Lock Down Publications: Facebook

Join Lock Down Publications/The New Era Reading
Group

Follow us on Instagram:

Lock Down Publications: Instagram

Email Us**: We want to hear from you!**

Submission Guideline.

Submit the first three chapters of your completed manuscript to ldpsubmissions@gmail.com, subject line: Your book's title. The manuscript must be in a .doc file and sent as an attachment. Document should be in Times New Roman, double spaced and in size 12 font. Also, provide your synopsis and full contact information. If sending multiple submissions, they must each be in a separate email.

Have a story but no way to send it electronically? You can still submit to LDP/Ca$h Presents. Send in the first three chapters, written or typed, of your completed manuscript to:

LDP: Submissions Dept
P.O. Box 944
Stockbridge, Ga 30281

DO NOT send original manuscript. Must be a duplicate.

Provide your synopsis and a cover letter containing your full contact information.

Thanks for considering LDP and Ca$h Presents.

Acknowledgments

I would like to thank God for such a raw talent, as well as my fans for all of the support. Much love to my people at Hobby behind the wall. I've received tons of love and support. Derrick and Del, I love you baby (free them guys). Momma, Granny, thank you for everything you instilled in me. Unc, Pops, I love you. If you haven't already, check out *Toe Tagz 1, 2, 3*. If you in my situation, just know it'll get greater later. Tomorrow has to come. If you got a dream, chase it, in spite of ya situation. I hope you enjoy my first romance novel: *Levels to This Shit*.

P.S. Lucia, thank you, baby.

Ah'Million

Prologue

The cool breeze sent chills down her arm. Syren should've been watching the live game in front of her. Instead, she was peering up at the sky. There were so many stars she could make a wish. That's what it seemed like on the cool summer night. It captured a mental picture, one she'd never forget. Staring at the beautiful sight made her forget about the baggage she carried every day that weighed her down. It gave her hope and peace, a feeling she didn't experience too often.

"Oooh, bitch, here come Maine and Dekari," Kreesha and Tonya voiced in a chipper tone.

Syren didn't know much about the two boys. She just recalled seeing them around periodically. Dudes hated them and the females flocked to them. She could tell they were getting a lot of paper, but she had other things on her mind, like making it through the day to get to tomorrow. Boys were the last thing on her mind. Besides, all they wanted was sex and Shelia would kill her if she found out she was being "fast", a term she used quite often when Syren did something she didn't approve of. To her it was simple, but Shelia was beyond petty.

"Hey Maine. Hey Dekari," the girls took turns speaking.

Syren looked past them as if it wasn't half-time and the game was still going on.

"Whaddup." They both nodded cooly.

Syren couldn't stand dudes with aloof personalities. *It's not even that serious*, she thought.

"Hey Syren," Maine voiced with a boyish grin.

She peered at him, dumbfounded, too shocked to respond.

"Say something," Kreesha whispered, nudging her in her side.

9

"Hi! I mean, hey Maine," Syren stammered right before he walked off. She cursed herself once he walked away smoothly. She did not want him to feel as if his presence moved her in any way. She was just amazed that he knew her name, since she and Maine never had a conversation.

"So you wasn't gon' tell us you and Maine cool?" Kreesha asked, crossing her arms at her chest.

"Kreesha, we have never exchanged words," Syren swore, lifting her right hand like she was about to take the stand.

"Whaaatt?" they both voiced in unison.

"He likes you then, Syren. Shoot your shot, bitch," Tonya urged.

"No, uh-uh! Hell no! Shelia not about to kill me."

"Girl, I'll fuck the shit out of him and Dekari, whichever one wants it first," Kreesha commented, groping herself.

"You so nasty, Kreesha." Syren scowled in disgust.

"Shit, I'm with Kreesha. Them niggas paid," Tonya agreed.

As the game went on, Syren occasionally cut her eyes at Maine. She didn't want him to be able to tell she was sneaking glances, so she continued to peer straight ahead and tried her damndest to see him out of the corner of her eye. The shit was starting to make her temples ache. A few times she was able to see him glancing into her direction, but she couldn't tell if he was looking directly at her or another chick in her path. Syren lifted her arms, pretending to stretch, tossing her hair over while turning her head in Maines's direction at the same time. He smirked at her mischievously as soon as their eyes met, as if he'd been waiting for her to look his way. Her heart raced and she quickly turned back around, pretending to watch the last few minutes of the fourth quarter. She was truly interested in the game, but kept drifting off to her thoughts -

thoughts of Maine. Tonya and Kreesha gossiped, yelling across the bleachers up until the last second of the game.

Syren's shoulders sagged like a champion boxer who'd just lost his title. She was quite upset that her school's team lost. She peered around awkwardly, waiting for Kreesha and Tonya to finish their conversations. They were the popular girls at school. Kreesha was known for doing everybody's hair and fighting, which was one of several reasons she flunked and had to repeat her senior year. Tonya was gorgeous - just trashy. She fucked and sucked dudes in vacant homes near the school and inside the boys' locker room. There was no shame in her lifestyle. She knew all the dudes 'cause they fucked her or wanted to fuck her, and she was beefing with damn near all the chicks because they envied her or wanted to beat her for fucking their man. Syren was the outcast: quiet, soft-spoken and drama free. Kreesha did drag her into it occasionally, and there were times Syren did fight only because she had to. She hated throwing hands, but when she did, Syren was something serious. Couldn't no female on God's green earth say they whooped her.

"Hold on, slow down," Maine said, catching up.

Syren slowed her stride while purposely avoiding eye contact. She didn't want to admit it, but something about his presence aroused her every time they were face to face.

"Hey, you think I can get your number or something so maybe we can link up? Just the two of us, someplace nice and quiet?"

She blushed at the offer. Maine smiled back, revealing his beautiful smile. He towered over her small frame. His eyes were mesmerizing and rare. You didn't see too many dark-skinned people with colored eyes. His honey-colored eyes reminded her of the caramel inside of a Twix. His skin was smooth and dark, enhancing his Colgate smile. He wore a

11

white and red Levi shirt, black N501's, and a pair of white Air Force Ones. He sported a lengthy gold chain with a nice-sized cross medallion. His wrist was bare, however, the ring on his pinky was massive and breathtaking.

"I'll call you. My mother is not cool," she responded, shaking her head.

"Don't have me waiting too long," he voiced, licking his succulent lips. He grabbed her hand, turned it over, and scribbled his number inside of her palm. He winked at her, then headed off in the direction of the concession stand, where Dekari was posted up waiting for him.

Syren stood there in disbelief. However, she wasn't too excited.

***

It had been three days since the night she got Maine's number, and she still hadn't called him.

It was mid-September. The weather was hotter than usual. Summer was beautiful and exciting, but Syren was more of a serene and cool breeze chick. She preferred winter. She sat with her legs crossed Indian style on her twin-sized bed. The hotter it got, the more she tampered with the fan in her window. She sang along to Aaliyah lyrics while carefully sewing the blue jeans. She was so focused that she stopped singing. Her mouth hung open unconsciously as she went to work, trying her damndest to imitate the shorts she'd seen earlier on an older chick from around the way.

"Sy," her mother began.

Syren's head jerked up in fear as her mother raced in hastily.

"Your ass better save all the legs on them jeans you cutting into shorts, 'cause I'm not buying no jeans come winter," her mother continued, peering at her from the doorway.

"Yes ma'am," Syren responded humbly in hopes to cease the nagging.

"I need you to walk to the store to get some eggs so I can start dinner." Her huge T-shirt swallowed her petite frame. It was evident she wasn't wearing a bra as her saggy breasts swung freely underneath the shirt.

"Yes mama," Syren answered obediently.

"I'm setting the money right here. Get a cartoon of eggs, a gallon of milk, and a loaf of bread," Shelia demanded.

"Momma, can I wear your Nikes?" Syren asked.

"Syren, you know your feet bigger than mine. I'm tired of you stretching my shoes out. You don't have to have swag just to walk down the street!" she hollered.

Sheila was right. Her feet were half a size, or perhaps an entire size, smaller than Syren's. Luckily she didn't have any corns on her toes. Syren was just adamant on wearing her mother's sneakers instead of her own. Shelia hadn't bought Syren any in almost two years. Syren did her best to take care of the shoes she had, cleaning them consistently to prevent wear and tear after so long. But Syren's Air Max's were beat up and she had an image to uphold. She lowered her head in shame, upset by her mother's reaction, and began to get dressed. Sheila watched her, instantly regretting her choice of words. If she couldn't afford new shoes, the least she could do was share hers, which she hardly wore.

At a young age, Syren lost her father to the streets. He was working as a janitor at the local elementary school. He was leaving when a younger guy ran up to him, disheveled and distraught, begging for help. Her father, being the caring and honorable man he was, tried calming the guy so he could get a clear understanding of what was going on. Out of nowhere, a car neared and shots were fired at both of them. Her mother explained to her that the young man owed the men a large sum of money. He had been running from them all night and once they finally caught up to him, they killed her father too, assuming he was a friend or family member. Shelia figured Syren would understand at her age, but here today, after eleven years, she still had yet to grasp an understanding of the reason behind her father's death. Things hadn't been right since then.

"Go on and get them shoes from underneath my bed," Sheila said in an attempt to lift Syren's spirit.

Syren gloated like a child in a candy store before running to retrieve the shoes.

The blazing sun burned the back of Syren's neck as she strolled down the sidewalk. She was feeling herself in the navy blue crop top and blue jean daisy dukes, clothes she had redesigned on her own. She stood in line at the store with her three items, waiting to pay for them, when she spotted Maine walk in. She shifted to her left leg, tapping her right foot impatiently.

"So you just not going to call a nigga?" he asked, stepping into her personal space.

Syren blushed, lowering her head.

His loud but smooth cologne heightened her senses. Maine knew Syren was trying to play hard to get. He eyed her lustfully. Her skin was flawless and golden. Her lips were pink and succulent. He eyed her exposed flesh. Her stomach was flat as a board and her ass was shaped like a bubble. She even had little hips. He noticed the shoes she had on were the same ones she wore to the game. They were fresh, yet they were seriously outdated. The shorts were homemade. He could tell by the strands that hung loosely. And her crop top was sexy because of the way it hugged her breasts, but the blue had faded tremendously, making the shirt look ashy. The minimal observation convinced Maine she was less fortunate.

"Let me get that for you," Maine insisted.

"No, I got it, Maine."

"Girl, give me that and go grab whatever else you want," he assured her.

"Nah, I'm fine," she responded, handing him the groceries and the two crumpled bills. She reached in her pocket to retrieve the change, ashamed to pull out the excessive change. She stood there just fishing around in her pocket.

"What you doing?" Maine said, eyeing her, confused.

"Getting the change."

"Nah, man, keep that. Go grab you a snack or two."

"Maine, no, I'm okay."

"Well, go grab me a bag of hot Funyons and a fruit punch jungle juice."

Syren did as Maine said and returned while he was placing the items on the countertop. He pulled out a wad of money, paid for the items, and headed out of the store.

"Thanks, Maine," Syren said, smiling from ear to ear.

"Come on. I'm about to give you a ride home."

The idea made Syren a bit uneasy, but she felt obliged after his act of kindness. Without uttering a word, she hopped in. The A/C in the metallic blue Crown Victoria blew superbly, better than the fan in her room. If she stayed a little further down the road, she might've fallen asleep. The rap music played at a high volume and the drums in the trunk hit so hard it rattled her thighs.

I could get used to this, she thought.

"Right here," she mumbled. The sight of the tiny apartment vexed Syren's spirit.

She reached for the door handle and Maine grabbed the opposite hand.

"Quit running and fuck with ya boy. Whether you know it or not, I been peeping you for a long time and I'm tired of playing games."

"I'm not ready for anything serious, Maine."

"Okay, that's cool, we can move slow. I don't like nothing fast but my money." He winked.

His skin was the color of a cup of chocolate milk. His hair was neatly trimmed and faded on the sides. His waves were deep and immeasurable. His lips were full and juicy. She could tell by the tint he smoked a lot of weed. His long lashes made his eyes appear smaller and his honey-colored irises were mesmerizing.

"That's my window right there. A lot of times I look out of it while I fantasize and listen to music. It's soothing to my soul."

Maine could look in Syren's eyes and discern her pain and struggles. "I'm a huge music fan too. When am I going to see you again?"

"I'll call you, Maine," she said, pulling the handle and climbing out. She looked back at him and waved right before stepping inside her house.

He pulled out of the lot, heading to his side of town. Guilt slowly consumed him as he thought about Skylar. She had been his bitch for years, but lately she'd been acting strange, and he wasn't feeling that. She was trying to manipulate and take advantage - ratchet shit.

"What's up, boy, what took you so long?" Dekari asked.

"Oh, I saw Syren at the gas station and gave her a ride home."

"That's what's up. You really like that li'l bitch, huh?"

"I do, but I really don't want to move too fast and steal her heart when I have Skylar."

"Check this out - and my OG's done told me this. When you got money, power, and respect, you're entitled to however many bitches you want. That's just one of the penalties they pay for fucking with a street nigga. They all gon' settle 'cause they know if they don't, the next bitch will. Understand? What bitch you know would turn down a life of luxury for love alone? You can have both. They can have whatever they heart desire. But just know I dib and dab from time to time. If I'm fulfilling my duty as a man, I should be able to fulfill any other desires as well. Whatever bitch that's not with it ain't worth it, 'cause they all replaceable. You don't tell them this, especially the few you truly care about. Just continue to tell them the lies they want to hear."

Maine let the words penetrate his mental and after a lot of thought, he slowly began to nod his head in agreement. Dekari was right.

Dekari and Maine had been friends since they were adolescents. They stayed in the same section in their apartment complex. Dekari was just a year older. He was the one that initially got them plugged in with the older cats. They could relate to one another because they both dealt with abandonment from their fathers. Being the only man in a house with females, they felt obliged to make a difference. They were two peas in a pod and alike in more ways than one.

"I'm going to pull up on you in a few hours. I'm about to holler at Skylar," Maine informed him before leaving.

Skylar answered the door in a sky blue thong and small baby doll T-shirt. The shirt hugged her breasts, revealing just a pinch of her tummy. The ring in her belly glistened whenever she moved.

"Hey bae."

"What's up, mama?" Maine responded, watching her ass jiggle with each step.

Skylar was the color of butter and thick in all the right places. She turned around, peering at him through her almond- · shaped eyes.

"Where you been, Maine?"

"With Dekari on the block."

"Well, I called Shalonda. She didn't see you."

"Come on, man, don't start picking. I don't feel all that," Maine said, waving her off.

"Yeah, whatever, nigga," she said, storming off.

Vibration caused Skylar's phone to slide across the table, instantly grasping his attention. He quickly picked it up to see who was calling. It was a text message from an unknown number. He tried opening it, but the screen changed, so he scrolled in to her inbox to see the text. He was taken aback when it showed her recent messages, and the last one was from him over an hour ago. *What the fuck?* he thought. Confused, he looked for the text again. Nothing.

"Now I know damn well I ain't going crazy," he whispered to no one in particular.

He texted a measly letter to her phone using his phone, just to see if he was tripping. Immediately the phone vibrated and he opened the text. He went through her messages again just to make sure the other text didn't magically appear, but there was nothing.

"Skylar!" Maine yelled. He was beyond frustrated. The vein in his forehead was beginning to protrude.

"What is it, Maine?" she answered, stopping directly in front of him with her hand on her hip.

"Ay, you got one of those hidden message apps?"

"What?" she asked with one of the ugliest scowls.

"Bitch, don't 'what' me. You heard me. Where it's at?"

18

"I don't have——"

"Say, check this: you lie again, and I'm gon' break the bone that keeps ya eye intact."

She smacked her lips before dropping her head.

"Go to it," he demanded, handing her the phone.

She tapped her screen a few times and tossed Maine the phone back.

"My calculator? Is that right?" He slowly nodded, his mouth turned downward, smirking while peering up at her.

"So where the messages at that were in here?"

"There weren't any," she lied through wide eyes.

"Come here," he stated in a low but serious tone.

When she was close enough he reached up and grabbed her lips, twisting and turning them mercilessly. She moaned and squirmed uncontrollably.

"Since you want to lie, I'ma rip these muthafuckas off," he said through clenched teeth.

Water filled her eyes, but it only made him inflict more pain. He used his nails to squeeze and yank on her lips. His jaws clenched tight, displaying the muscle in them. He finally shoved her backward when he noticed the blood on his fingertips.

Skylar's lips ached so badly. She rubbed her jaw instead, afraid to make direct contact. She was trying to say something, but it sounded like gibberish. Tears streamed down her face, instantly irritating the open wounds, causing them to burn. She squeezed her eyes shut, but it was too painful.

Maine walked out and slammed the door shut. He hopped in his Vic and cruised the streets to clear his head. He bypassed Syren's apartment and decided to turn around. He parked outside her apartment, peering at her window, but her blinds were closed. *She's probably asleep,* he thought. *Or listening to music.*

19

"Fuck it!" he said aloud, stepping out of his car. He jogged to her window carefully, looked around, then tapped a few times with his car key.

Seconds later, she appeared, looking dumbfounded. A huge grin formed once she realized it was him. Her thick hair was all over her head, but it didn't take away from her beauty.

"Come on, let's go to the Waffle House," he said as soon as she opened the window high enough to hear him.

"Maine, I can't leave. I'm scared. What if my momma calls me for something? I love the Waffle House, but I don't want to get in trouble." Her eyes were so innocent, but he could tell by her mouth that she wasn't.

"Alright, I'll see you around." He jogged away.

He heard her say something, but he didn't bother turning around. He hopped in his car and sped off, only to return a short time later with food. He knocked on Syren's window. This time, she really looked stunned.

"I brought you something." He grinned, holding the Waffle House bag up.

She grinned back, then reached for the bag.

"Damn, can I join you at least?"

She peered behind her, then removed the fan, giving him access to climb in.

He climbed in one leg at a time, holding the crotch of his pants as he stepped inside.

The room was tiny and devoid of much furniture. A blanket was taking the place of the curtains. A small flat screen TV was placed on top of the night stand. The brown paint was chipped and one of the legs was broken. He focused his attention on her instead of her old-fashioned decor.

"I thought you were upset. That was so sweet of you to bring me something to eat," she said, hugging his waist tightly. Syren was about four inches shorter than him. He

20

grinned while peering at her closely, taking in her natural beauty. "You didn't get yourself anything?" she asked in between bites.

"Nah, I'm not hungry, baby girl."

His phone rang, scaring both of them. He quickly silenced it, but only seconds later, he had to silence it again.

"Who's that?" she pried

"Damn, you nosy," he laughed. "It's my girl."

The statement crushed Syren's spirits. She tried acting cool, but the jealousy was evident. "Oh, you got a girl?"

"Yeah, but she won't have her position for too long."

Hearing that was music to her young ears. "But she has one now," she spoke in a low tone, closing the container on her food.

"Don't let the small shit bother you. I want you, Syren, but I just have to find out if I can trust you. I'm an important guy and I can't have just anyone around me, but if you hop on board, I'll treat you like the only woman in the world and give you the desires of your heart."

Maine leaned in for a kiss. He knew if she kissed him back the deal was sealed. He placed his full lips against hers. When she slid her warm tongue inside of his mouth, the rest was history.

Twelve years later, they were still going steady.

Chapter 1
The Beginning

"Hello?" Syren answered, unable to cease the sniffles.

"Quit crying and go to sleep. Jermaine won't be coming home tonight," the woman on the other end of the phone retorted.

"Who the hell is this?" Syren screamed into the receiver. Veins protruding from her neck as she felt the blood rush to her face. She listened to the woman closely, trying to decipher the familiarity in her voice.

"Don't worry about all of th——"

"Hey!" a male in the background chimed in, cutting her short.

Click!

Swear I cannot win for losing
I been out here being faithful
I always got this on lockdown
But that ain't keepin' us stable
So I guess I know what I got to do
Give you a taste of your own medicine, hey, yeah...

The drops of rain descended in abundance, crashing into Syren's vehicle. It could be heard over the Summer Walker lyrics that played softly as she sped through the quiet but busy streets of Dallas in her maroon Dodge Challenger. She removed the phone from her ear, staring at the screen in sheer disbelief. Her heart raced like a repeat felon's with a trunk full of dope being chased by the police. Never in the years of being involved with Jermaine had a female called her phone or contacted her in any form period.

She awoke in the wee hours of the night to find his side of the bed empty for the second time this week. Usually she'd wait up for him to arrive, ready to hear another lie, but this time she refused. Tears streamed down her cheeks while she peered straight ahead, squinting to see past the heavy rain. "This the last straw. It's over for Jermaine's ass," she spoke aloud, trying to convince herself.

Tired was an understatement. She was sick of him. They'd been together for twelve years and engaged a little over a year. Despite the recent bullshit, he was the perfect father to their son Jaelyn and materialistically, he gave her everything her heart desired. But for some reason, he couldn't afford to give her the most inexpensive item of them all: loyalty.

For two years now, Jermaine had been showing signs of infidelity. The change in his behavior and schedule compelled her to make such assumptions. It had started out innocent and petty, nothing detrimental and overwhelming.

Syren raced home like a NASCAR driver, disregarding stop signs and red lights as she envisioned packing all of his shit and throwing it into the street. She swerved around the corner and her mouth dropped at the sight of Jermaine's truck parked in the driveway.

"What in the hell?" she mouthed soundlessly, parking beside his truck. Agitated, she entered, then peered around, the two-story home. She scanned the kitchen area and dining room, but no luck. She climbed the steps two at time and entered the bedroom, spotting a sleeping Jermaine, who lay comfortably on his stomach.

"Jermaine!" she yelled, flicking on the light switch. He didn't budge. Enraged, she shook him violenty, startling him.

"What's up, baby?" he mumbled, squinting at her through one eye.

"Don't 'what's up, baby' me! Where have you been, Maine?" she hollered, hovering over him. Syren visualized herself clawing his eyes out, she was so upset.

"You couldn't wait for me to wake up for this?" he asked, peering up at her seriously.

"For this? The nerve of you! Tell me where you been! I've been roaming the streets looking for you and here you are questioning me like I'm irritating you," she voiced, appalled by his reaction.

"Syren Janae, go shower and get in this bed. After leaving the office, I stopped by Dekari's to fill him in on the vacancies being destroyed. It's those damn junior high kids sneaking over during school hours," he explained, positioning himself on his elbows.

Syren didn't know if Jermaine was lying or telling the truth. She wanted to believe him, but the disturbing call was too convincing.

"Okay, even if all that is true…who is this chick that called my phone, Maine?"

"I have no idea. What bitch? Don't no one have any business contacting you. What did she say?" He sat up, appearing dumbfounded.

" 'Jermaine isn't coming home tonight'," Syren mocked with confidence.

"Uh, I'm pretty sure if you would've stayed on the line, Tommy would've revealed himself."

"Tommy? Who the hell is Tommy?"

"Nephew Tommy with the *Steve Harvey Show*," he admitted, laughing uncontrollably.

Syren fumed.

"I'm saying it has to be a joke because I'm here in the flesh, baby!" Maine joked.

"I hate you, and when I do catch your dirty dick behind, I'm done. You're going to need Jesus, Tommy, your mother, and whoever else. Which still won't be enough," Syren voiced through clenched teeth before storming off to the shower.

"Syren!" Jermaine called out.

But she ignored him. Instead, she removed her wet clothes and climbed into the shower. Tears silently streamed down Syren's face as she stood under the steaming hot water. She roughly scrubbed her skin, mumbling sinister things under her breath. She wanted so badly for Jermaine to join her. Minutes later, she stepped out of the shower. Just as she expected, Jermaine was out like a light. She glared at him, discreetly scoping for his phone. However, it wasn't anywhere in sight. Drained and jaded, she lay on her side of the bed, still as a board.

***

The next morning, Syren and Jaelyn were headed out the door when Dekari pulled into the driveway. Jaelyn was twelve years old with NBA dreams. He wasn't talkative or nerve-wracking. He just wanted to hoop and play video games.

Dekari stepped out of his 2019 Lincoln. He always looked so appealing. Dekari and Jermaine used to hustle together illegally, at first. Now they owned an entire apartment complex and had been legit ever since.

"Good morning, Syren. What's up, Jaelyn?" Dekari greeted.

"Hey De! You still taking me to the Bucks and Mavericks game?" Jaelyn asked, clutching his basketball.

"Of course. It's this weekend. So make sure you're ready," Dekari answered, brushing Jaelyn's hair with the palm of his hand.

"Hey De, was Jermaine with you last night?" Syren asked.

He hesitated for a moment before saying, "Yeah, he was."

Dekari lied for Maine all the time. She didn't even know why she wasted her time asking. People who didn't know Dekari and Maine always assumed they were brothers because they both were dark-skinned. Dekari was just a shade or two darker. His color put you in the mind of the chocolate in the nutella jar: smooth and rich. He had a set of deep dimples and an award-winning smile. His bald fade was always fresh and so was his swag.

This fool always licking his lips like he Michael Vick or somebody, she thought.

The Chanel Bleu cologne invaded her nostrils and rattled her insides as he bypassed her, which he would've never guessed since Syren never looked back or slowed her stride.

Syren watched Jaelyn shift uncomfortably in his seat out of the corner of her eye. He hated her choice of music.

"Momma, I'm going to the recreation center to play ball after school!" he yelled over the music.

Syren turned the volume down and said, "Okay, that's fine. Walk to your grandmother's when you're done."

Jaelyn was the spitting image of Maine. He had his thick brows and long eyelashes. He even had his honey-colored eyes. Jaelyn's shoulder-length dreads were the only difference.

"I'm just a ghetto man living in this ghetto town..."

She turned up the volume while singing along to the blues song when she felt Jaelyn tap her arm. She quickly turned the volume down, giving him her undivided attention.

"Ma, can you keep that down since we almost in front of my school?" he asked with pleading eyes.

"There's nothing you should be ashamed of. Luckily you're not walking or on the bus!" Syren retorted, immediately turning the volume up, veering into the lane in front of his school.

Jaelyn rolled his eyes and slouched in his seat. Once Syren's Challenger came to a stop, Jaelyn climbed out, peering back at Syren disapprovingly.

"Hey Jaelyn!" Two girls walking inside of the school building yelled.

"What's up," Jaelyn mumbled with his head down, walking away from the car.

Syren knew Jaelyn was ashamed of the old music, but she didn't care. She felt like Maine was allowing Jaelyn to grow up too fast by letting him listen to the new rap music that tainted children's minds, and he wasn't even a teenager yet. Jaelyn despised her, but enjoyed being around his father because Jermaine let him do what he wanted to do.

Syren sped off and headed towards her salon. Minutes later, she pulled up to the salon she and Maine had purchased three years ago. At thirty years old, Syren was quite successful. She had her own home and two cars. She didn't owe Uncle Sam or anyone else and her credit was A-1.

Traffic around the shop was light, yet it was still pretty early. Deon was posted up, as usual.

"Hey Syren, I got that new Drake and Wayne," he said, leaning up against the wall.

"Deon, ain't nobody listening to CD's no more!"

Deon would sell the shirt off his back if you offered to buy it. He was fairly handsome. He wore a lot of knock-offs, which was a turn-off.

"Check this out then. She's new and she the truth. Just give me ten?"

The title seemed interesting. She eyed the cover and the back. The cover art was dope. "Okay, I'll take it," she said, retrieving the ten dollars from her purse and handing it to Deon.

He immediately walked away in the opposite direction.

Syren purchased all sorts of books from Deon to add to the shelf inside the salon for her customers to read while waiting. If they weren't able to finish it and wanted to, she allowed them to purchase it.

"Hey! When you get some more Febreze and Tide pods, come pay me a visit!" she called out.

"I got you! Give me ten minutes!" he yelled

"Hey y'all," Syren greeted, walking inside the shop.

Four stylists including herself worked in the salon. She quickly peered around, noticing everyone was in attendance except Kreesha.

"Good morning, Syren," Angie said as Syren bypassed her. At the age of forty-six, Angie was the oldest of the crew. Her clients were older women who rocked short cuts and bobs or preferred wigs. That's why today, Syren found it completely odd seeing a younger woman in her chair. Some of their features were similar, so Syren assumed they were related.

Still upset from the incident last night, she headed straight to the back to her small but neat office. Syren hurried out when she heard a loud commotion.

"I want my money back!" the petite pecan-colored woman voiced loudly.

Syren's eyes grew wide as she looked on, appalled.

"Ma'am? Um…what seems to be the problem?" Syren asked, folding her arms in front her.

"Um…" the woman mocked. "The problem is, you got this antique stylist up in here! I told her to barely bump my ends, and she done took it upon herself to put these tight-ass flips in my hair!" she yelled, peering at Syren disapprovingly.

"Yeah, I'm older, but your young ass better hope you look this good once you reach my age. If you reach my age!" Angie shot back.

"Lady! Flips not in. This 2020. You fucking up my swag!" the lady, who looked to be in her mid-twenties, yelled.

Angie and the lady continued going back and forth when Syren intervened, handing her sixty dollars.

"Have a nice day, ma'am," Syren said, flashing a bogus smile.

"Yeah, have a nice day," Angie mocked.

"Hey y'all! Sorry I'm late." Kreesha walked in, bypassing the chick walking out. Kreesha eyed her until she was outside. "Who was she? Why she look all stank in the face?" Kreesha asked, peering at Angie and Syren.

"Girl, you tripping," Syren assured her. If Kreesha had known what really occurred, she would've chased the chick down.

Kreesha was Syren's older cousin. She was loud and quick to throw hands. Before working in the shop, she was tied into a few illegal dealings. Nothing major, but enough to cause her to spend some time behind bars. She was older than Syren, but acted younger. She was also one of the baddest stylists in the salon. Ratchet for sure, but hilarious as hell. Everyone loved Kreesha. Days in the shop without her were long and dull.

Kreesha was a little on the chunky side. She had a lot of ass to go with everything else. She was very flamboyant and also messy and dramatic - never to Syren, but to others. She had straight white teeth, high cheekbones, and pencil thin eyebrows that she filled in. Her reddish-brown skin was covered in tattoos.

"Cuz you already know!" Kreesha spoke indirectly, placing her bags down in her booth.

"Layla and Shunda stopped by looking for you," Uh'Nija chimed in.

"Okay. Let's go to the office. I got so much to tell you!"

Ah'Million

Chapter 2
Niggas ain't shit

Maine poured the coffee into his cup, glaring out the window of his office.

"So how about this bitch Uh'Nija phoned Syren last night?" he spoke in between sips.

"She what?" Dekari asked, wide-eyed.

"Yep, she did. I'm assuming private."

"What happened?"

"Syren asked me about it. I told her it had to have been Nephew Tommy."

"Ahhh! You a fool!" Dekari burst into laughter. He laughed until tears welled up in his eyes, bending over and clutching his stomach.

"That shit not funny. There's the UPS dude. Open the door."

Dekari opened the door to the office inside the Falls apartments that he and Maine owned. There was no manager or assistant manager. Dekari and Maine owned and ran the place. They figured the less people they had to pay, the more money they would make. However, Maine did hire an office clerk, a Caucasian lady named Susan. Susan was up in age and definitely unattractive. Syren would snoop around all the time if she was young and attractive, so to minimize the drama, Maine chose Susan. Dekari was upset about the choice, but quickly got over it.

Syren normally visited twice a week at the most. Most of her time was spent at the salon. Since the opening of the salon, Syren had become so reserved and conservative. Usually, the clerk would take an extra lunch break, allowing the privacy for a nice quick sex session, but lately, all of that had ceased.

"About time," Dekari voiced loudly, referring to the pole while rubbing his hands together.

"Shit! I almost forgot. Tell him to set it up in the back, on your side," Maine ordered. Although he loved Syren with all of his heart, the spark between them had died. He missed the *hot and the ready* Syren, the *wake up to head and breakfast in bed* Syren, *the daredevil and roleplay* Syren. Even all of that didn't mean he'd be one hundred percent faithful, but at least he would be full - full of Syren. When you're full of something, there's no room for anything else.

Lately he had become sloppy with the profit - not in the sense of money, but in his marriage. Uh'Nija wasn't the first chick he messed around with, and from the looks of it, she wouldn't be the last. Maine was a typical man. Whenever that monster between his legs jumped, switched, or rattled, he reacted in ways that were not appeasing to his wife.

"Hey," Maine spoke into the phone.

"Heeey bae," Un'Nija answered cheerfully.

"Come to the office"

"The office? This early? I must've been superb last night! You don't ever call requesting my presence this early."

"Just hurry up."

"Okaaay."

Click.

Un'Nija was a resident inside the Falls Apartments. She was beautiful, medium brown, with a body full of tattoos. She had a perfect set of teeth that complemented her smile, Standing at 5'8", she was taller than most. She had a model physique. Everything was slim except her voluptuous ass. Everyone thought it was natural, but the only natural thing about Un'Nija was her eye color. Her C-cup breasts were fake also.

Uh'Nija was just trash - not the garbage inside of the dumpster, but the juice at the very bottom. Other than being a slut, Uh'Nija was a drama queen and ratchet. She had no goals or achievements. Her only accomplishment was the fact that she worked at Syren's nice, high-end salon.

"Hey boo!" she yelled excitedly, walking into the office, tossing her black and blonde box braids over her shoulder.

"Come to the back," Maine demanded

Uh'Nija peered at him with mischievous and lust-filled eyes while following him to the back. The back was divided into two rooms: one for Maine and one for Dekari. Only a love seat, desk, and shelf decorated the small office space. There were no windows inside either private office. The space wasn't technically intended for what it had transformed into. A printer and laptop were on the desk, portraying a perfect office scene, but there was more occurring than setting appointments and faxing papers.

"Yes daddy," she said, walking inside and closing the door behind her.

"Let me holla at you," he demanded, turning on his heels so that they were face to face.

"Huh?" she asked, grinning.

Whack!

The open palm connecting with her cheek caused Uh'Nijas head to snap.

"Hell nah!" she yelled, charging Maine wildly.

"Ay, chill!"

Whack!

Maine hadn't intended to hit Un'Nija for the second time, but he became frustrated with the kicking and screaming.

"For real, Maine?" she asked in disbelief, holding her burning cheek.

"Hell yeah for real! What you thought was going to happen? Syren is off limits. Don't ever call my wife. Oh, and if I find out you in there throwing lugs out, discussing shit about me and you with your coworkers, I'm going to whack yo' ass."

"Okay, Maine, but I wouldn't do anything like that. I would never bring heat to us! I love you, and sometimes I just want you all to myself," she pleaded with her hands clasped in front of her.

"You fucked up big time. My wife is my everything and if I lose her because of you, I'll lose it," Maine stated seriously, glaring down at her venomously.

"I can be your everything," she said, moving towards him seductively while undressing.

"If you undress, I'm going to throw your ass out as is. Remain dressed and dismiss yourself."

Loathingly, Uh'Nija glared at him for what felt like hours, but it was merely a few seconds. She walked out, slamming both doors to each section of the office shut.

Maine and Dekari had decided to order a stripper pole for entertainment while enduring the long and boring days in the office. Maine stood peering out the window of the front office while the guy set the pole up.

"Mr. Wiley, what did you order?"

"Susan, mind your business. Your job is to greet applicants, answer the phone, and set appointments. Anything other than that is above your job description and pay rate. Meaning it doesn't pertain to you." Susan was just a little too nosy for Maine's liking.

"Yes sir." She smiled coyly.

He knew she was bad mouthing him in her mind, but he was fine with that as long as she kept it to herself.

"So you saw these new chicks that moved in apartment 1202?" Maine asked, redirecting his attention.

"Black and Yellow?" Dekari questioned.

"Huh? That's their names?" Maine scowled

"Nah, that's just a name I have for them. Shit. One is black and the other is yellow," he explained.

Dekari and Maine had been boys for a long time, years before he met Syren. They lived in the same apartments and went to the same school. They got suspended from school and ended up at the same alternative school. Although Maine stayed in trouble as a young'un, he was the brains. Everyone knew not to fuck with Dekari and Maine. Dekari was the fighter, the hothead. Anything made him snap. He kept them in shit, whether it was at home or school.

***

Village Oaks, 1996

Dekari and Maine were chilling on the stoop plotting on a way they could get the money to buy the new Jordans that were scheduled for release tomorrow. They were fourteen years of age during the summer of their eighth grade year. The sun was blazing, forcing scowls upon their faces as they peered around the poverty-stricken apartments.

Using his hands as shields to keep the sun away, Maine said, "Man, if we don't get them J's, they gon' really know we ain't standing on shit."

"I got a plan. It's a little risky, but it just might work," Dekari added while smirking.

Maine could tell by the smirk on his face that he had some mischievous shit going on. "What's up?" Maine asked curiously.

"Well, my momma buys these cheap-ass white tea candles from Family Dollar. I'm going to snatch like three of them, pull the little string out, and cut it up like crack."

"That shit not going to work, man."

"I'll be back," Dekari said, running inside the house.

Maine waited on the stoop in front of his grandmother's house for Dekari. There was no way in hell the fiends were going to fall for this. Maine spotted the ice cream truck nearing, so he hopped off the stoop and jogged towards the truck. He waved his hand calmly until he came to a stop.

The driver acted as if he didn't notice Maine at first. All the while he was hoping to see someone - anyone. "What would you like?" he asked in his thick accent.

"A bag of hot Cheetos and two Fruit Roll Ups."

"Hey, get some of them baggies," Dekari blurted, pointing at the different and multi-colored baggies. The extremely small bags resembled bite-sized sandwich bags. Dekari waited for Maine on the stoop, removing the candles from his pocket.

"This shit better work. These damn bags $2.50," Maine complained, rolling them onto his lap.

"I got this. Just ride with me," Dekari assured him.

"Here." Maine handed him a Fruit Rollup and Dekari went to work. Maine didn't know what dope looked like, but looking at the product Dekari had, it appeared pretty legit.

"Come on, this twenty dime rocks. We just can't sell them in one spot 'cause once they take a hit, it's over," he stated seriously.

They footed it to the car wash up the street. Maine's heart pumped rapidly with each step. He was anxious and nervous all at once.

"It's hotter then two fat bitches sitting side by side in a sauna," Maine voiced, wiping the sweat from his forehead.

"It's right there," Dekari pointed. "Hurry up. I don't see none of those niggas from the Butta Beans up there."

They jogged to the car wash. Fiends were all over the place.

"We sell one pack, and the rest will sell itself," Dekari preached.

Maine didn't know exactly what he meant by that until he sold the first rock. Seconds later, the fiends swarmed the boys like celebrities.

"My brothas, let me wash them for a piece of that in your pocket!" the fiend spoke through extremely chapped lips. His beady eyes roamed the boys from head to toe.

"Wash what?" Dekari asked.

"Them... Them Jordans o-on your feet" he stuttered, pointing directly at his shoes.

"Hell nawl, these ain't no rims!" Dekari shot back

"You eyeing us like you want to jack some'. Ain't nobody taking shit over here, my boy," Maine cut in, lifting his T-shirt and revealing the black handle.

"You trippin', youngblood," he said, backing away, nearly tripping over his own two feet. He should've been trying to wash his own shoes, since they looked like a pair someone tied together and threw on the cable line.

"Come on, fam, it done got quiet. They must be at the back testing out that wax."

"Hell yeah. Let's go before they realize it's bullshit," Maine said.

"Let's post up at Kwik Check."

Kwik Check was the neighborhood mom and pop store and was family owned by a Vietnamese family.

"How many left?" Maine asked.

"Just four."

They hung around the store for ten minutes before realizing it was useless. They headed back to Village Oaks, and along the way, they were able to pop two more, then pop the last two in their very own apartments.

"I told you, boy," Dekari bragged, grinning.

"That shit was easy!" Maine shot back, dapping him up.

"Here." Dekari handed Maine his half, stuffing the money into his jeans. Dekari said, "Tomorrow we gon' catch the bus to Foot Locker and——"

A loud commotion compelled him to stop speaking so he could hear better.

"What's that?" Maine asked, peering around wide-eyed.

"Let's go check it out," Dekari suggested, standing to his feet, pulling up his jeans.

"You take yo' 'let's go check it out' looking ass over there. I'm staying right here."

"Scary ass."

"Yeah, you can call me scary, cool. Call me any and everything but broke, nigga!" Maine clapped back.

Dekari waved Maine off and headed towards the commotion.

"There he go!" someone yelled.

Without looking up, Maine knew they were talking about Dekari. He wanted to run inside on his dumb ass, but his feet wouldn't move.

"Come on, man, we got to go. It's like three of those fiends back there!" Dekari yelled, bending the corner.

Maine hopped up to join him, only to run into Big Mike. Big Mike ran the Oak. h

He was an O.G.

"Whoa, what y'all li'l niggas up to?" he asked with a puzzled expression plastered across his handsome but chubby face.

"Them fiends——" Dekari was in the middle of explaining when the angry crowd led by the fiends hit the corner.

"What the fuck going on? What y'all done did?" he voiced to no one in particular, peering around wide-eyed.

"They sold us fake rocks!" Ann hollered, leading the pack. Ann stayed in the apartments. Dudes would give her rocks and she would buy it, suck and fuck…whatever you requested for the pipe.

"Y'all motherfukas not going to fuck with them and I said that," Big Mike announced, removing the. 40 from his waist. "Ann, yo' clucked-out ass know these boys. You know damn well they don't have no work"

"Well, I thought you put them——"

"Put them on? You a damn fool. This not *New Jack City*, bitch. These kids, and all y'all funky asses that bought that shit gon' take that loss, straight up."

The crowd slowly cleared out. Maine and Dekari were relieved.

"Thanks, Big Mike." Both the boys spoke in unison.

"Look, y'all can't be doing no raunchy shit like that. What if I wasn't in there fucking my bitch? Them fiends work hard for pennies so they can get their fix. They'll kill you behind that rock. Don't do that anymore. Go get you a lawnmower and cut some yards or wash some cars."

"You right," Maine agreed.

"Yes sir," Dekari responded.

Since that day forward, Maine came up with all the schemes. Dekari's always led them to trouble.

***

Angie hit the alarm on her 2018 Ford Focus and dashed inside. She had left the shop a little later than usual, which gave her very little time to prepare Brandon's meal.

"Ouch!" she yelped, grabbing her skinned knee. It was now pink from the impact of crashing into the concrete slab after trying to climb the porch quickly.

Once she made it inside the house she and Brandon shared, she dropped her keys and purse and jogged into the kitchen. She moved like Tina Turner on *What's Love Got To Do With It*, the scene where she was packing her shit. Cooking utensils and empty containers occupied the countertop. The sound of keys jingling could be heard from afar. Angie began moving quicker. Her trembling hands were evidence that she was terror-stricken.

"Angie!" Brandon called out.

"Yes, I'm in the kitchen, baby!"

"Hey baby, it smells good in here. What you cook?" he asked, burying his face in the crease of her neck. His strong arms wrapped tightly around her waist and he used his massive hands to squeeze her ass.

"Well, I'm making pork chops, mashed potatoes, mac and cheese, and sweet honey rolls," she spoke delightedly. Angie was so cheerful that Brandon wasn't in his usual foul mood.

"Okay. I'm going to shower. Today was an extremely long day," he said softly, pecking her on the lips.

Whew! She exhaled in relief as soon as she heard the door to the bedroom shut. Brandon's temper was unreal. Some nights she was afraid to sleep next to him.

Brandon never returned to the kitchen. Instead, he went into the den, where he watched ESPN. She strolled inside and handed him the plate of food. There wasn't a thank you, friendly gesture, or hint of appreciation. Filling her lungs with the stale air, she inhaled deeply to rid herself of frustration. Angie had grown used to the multi-personalities.

"You going to just stand there and watch me eat?" He peered up at her distastefully. His eyes were mysterious and free of emotion, forcing her to lower her head. She could never look at him and assume his thoughts or emotions.

"I just wanted to make sure you liked it" she voiced in a low tone before returning back to the kitchen. She rested against the countertop, trying to gather her thoughts, when Brandon strolled in, invading her space. She shivered at the sight of him. He didn't look too pleased and the plate he held was covered with food.

"Taste this" he demanded calmly.

"Taste what?" Angie asked, dumbfounded, while backing away.

"This!" he yelled, stuffing the pork chop inside her mouth. "You taste that? Where's the seasoning, Angie? You used it all up for that nigga, didn't you?"

The simmering pork chop scalded her lips as soon as it connected with her mouth. She squirmed while gripping his arm in an attempt to cease the madness, but she was no match for his strength. Tears descended down her face as she attempted to yell, but the porkchop muffled her screams. Finally dropping his arm, he palmed her face, shoving her backwards into the stove.

"Aagghh!" she yelped. Apparently she had never gotten the chance to cut the stove off and the sting from the blazing stove made her dance like Michael and holler like Prince. She waved and waggled her hand back and forth for some relief. She peered at Brandon, who stood there watching her through vacan't eyes while she struggled immensely she quickly opened the freezer and placed her hand on top of a frozen bag of French fries.

He took the plate that was in the opposite hand and tossed it on the counter. Mac and cheese and mashed potatoes tipped off the side and onto the counter.

"I'm going to go get me something to eat" he proclaimed, disappearing around the corner.

"Whew!" she voiced, taking a few deep breaths before removing her hand. She wiped the grease from her lips and headed into the bathroom, where she retrieved the first aid kit. She examined her hand carefully. The burn wasn't too bad but it was visible. Angie was happy to have burned her hand rather than have to face his wrath. Before the burn, she had peered into his eyes. He wasn't done. He wasn't satisfied. He didn't inflict enough pain. He wanted her to suffer. The burn was simply perfect for his liking.

She knew Brandon loved her. He just had a weird way of showing it. He loved her for her. No other man would ever love all 196 pounds of her. Her saggy breasts and barely plump ass weren't imperfections to him. Angie wasnt ashamed of either asset since he was willingly attentive to each and every body part. He even loved her discolored asshole. She was yellow as the yellow brick road and her butthole was as black as coal. He had no problem sucking all eleven of her toes, typical birth defects. However, the corn on her pinky toe was a totally different story. Unlike all the rest of them, he wasn't forcing Angie to have surgery.

Once Angie wrapped her hand with the brown Ace bandage, she cleaned up the kitchen. In less than twenty minutes, the loud music from the driveway startled her. She was afraid he might like to finish the abuse. She ran and slid underneath the covers on top of their king-sized mattress. Her heart was beating so fast she was sure it'd bust.

As soon as the front door slammed, she shut her eyes to pretend to be asleep. She could feel her lids jumping. She continued to squeeze them shut. She lay underneath the covers, still as a board, afraid any sudden movement might result in a beating. Hearing the water from the shower calmed her spirit, and it wasn't long before she drifted off to sleep - without a shower.

Ah'Million

Chapter 3
Sex isn't better than love

"Boy, you lucky I do my own hair, 'cause your ass would be broke if you had to fix this every time you mess it up," Kreesha joked with Chris. She attempted to fix her messy ponytail while eyeing him lustfully.

Sex with Chris was exciting and refreshing. He made her feel twenty-one again. The attraction between them was immeasurable and there were times he couldn't contain himself. Wherever and whenever that penis rose, he made her legs unfold, and Kreesha enjoyed it just as much as he did. She wasn't used to the aggressive sexual demands, which made things so renewing and desirous. She pulled her jeans up before climbing over the armrest and into the passenger seat, removing the strands of hair that were stuck to her forehead.

"Give me a kiss," he demanded.

Their lips locked and Chris kissed her viciously, as if he wanted to tear her clothes off with his teeth. Kreesha returned the same emotion.

"Let me stop before I have to park this car again," Chris voiced as he pulled away from her lips.

Chris was ten years older than Kreesha, however, it didn't take away from his appearance. He dressed expensively and casually. His mocha-colored skin complemented his bright eyes. His goatee was always lined to perfection. The few grey strands didn't symbolize just his age, but it exemplified wisdom, which separated the boys from the men. His full lips and bald fade really turned her on.

Chris and Kreesha met a month ago at a car auction. She later found out Chris owned six cars and was into real estate. Four of the cars they'd had sex in. Today made it number five, and it was very amazing inside the spacious Cadillac Escalade.

"You hungry?" he asked, never taking his eyes off the road.

"You know sex gives me an appetite."

"Baby, everything gives you an appetite. It's cool; you're my chunky butt," he joked, slightly pinching her cheek.

"I want to see if you really have skills."

"Sure, we can do that. I have been telling you I can throw down. Now it's time I show you."

Chris's phone rang before Kreesha could respond.

"Hello?" he answered in his deep and demanding voice. "Oh, hi Ms. Livingston, how may I help you?" he asked while signaling Kreesha to turn the music down. "Yes, the house on Brine is still available. Well, I'm actually busy at the moment with family, but if you're still available in thirty minutes, I can meet you there. Okay, great, I'll see you then."

Click.

"Yes!" Chris cheered. "Bae, I promise to cook for you next time. For now, can we just go to a restaurant?"

"Sure, bae, I know you're a businessman." Kreesha was excited merely because Chris was joyful himself. She loved the fact that her man was so successful, but she truly felt that their relationship lacked quality time.

"Olive Garden?" he asked.

"That's fine."

They veered into the spacious lot. Several restaurants decorated it as well as several cars. Hand in hand, they strolled inside. The lights were dim, the place was half-empty, and the waitress that served them was gorgeous.

While enjoying their meals, Kreesha asked Chris, "Bae, why do you always eat with one hand?" She watched him struggle to butter his roll.

"I was raised that way, so it has become a habit. My mother was big on the whole no elbows on the table thing and

48

it was always these elbows that would end up on the table, so after so many beatings, I just started eating with one arm."

"Ďang, I thought my mother was strict."

"Would you like something to go? I don't mean to seem antsy, but I am a little excited."

"No, hunny, let's go so you can handle your business," she stated, waving her hand for the check.

"Kreesha, you're beautiful inside and out. I'm so glad I met you." Chris always had something sweet on his lips.

"The feeling is mutual, boo," she said as they headed back to the other side of town to drop her off.

***

"Okay, now I'm going to show you and then teach you a move called the butterfly."

Syren deeply exhaled, correcting her posture. She didn't know that pole tricks required so much. She lacked stamina and strength.

"Stand beside the pole and wrap the back of your leg around the pole. Jump up, then open and close your legs as the pole spins around. If you have a pole that doesnt automatically spin, this move is a bit more difficult - just a tad bit," the instructor explained.

Syren had been discreetly attending pole lessons for three weeks now. She would go while Maine was busy at the office. She figured she needed to begin making efforts to spice things up. Maine hadn't admitted it, but she knew he was messing around.

"Syren, you lack upper body strength, which you will need to be able to pull yourself up. Either gain muscle or lose weight. In this class, you're going to do both. You don't have to go on a strict diet, but change some of those bad eating habits."

"Okay, it's getting a little late. I'll see you Thursday."

"Okay, drive safely."

Syren waved goodbye to everyone and headed home.

Lost in her thoughts, Syren thought of different ways to captivate and maintain her fiancé's attention like she used to. She carefully stepped out of her car. Her legs ached and burned with each step. Surprisingly, Maine's car was in the driveway.

"Wheeww!" She exhaled loudly, hoping to obtain someone's attention, but no one heard her. *I guess*, she thought, wincing at the pain in her legs as she climbed the stairs.

"Hey baby," she said cheerfully, peeking inside Jaelyn's room.

"Hey Momma," he responded dryly.

Jaelyn and Syren never had a normal mother and son bond. He treated her like the stepchild and his father like a god. She knew it was because she set the rules and enforced them, unlike his dad, who never told him no, making Syren look like the bad guy. She closed the door to his room and slipped inside her own, instantly spotting a jumpy Jermaine. He slipped his phone underneath the pillow. Syren dropped her head, pretending she didn't see the sneaky movement.

"Hey hunny," he greeted her, lying on top of the covers fully clothed.

"Where you going?"

"Nowhere. I just got here. I was waiting for you to pull up so we can shower together, then chill and enjoy a little quality time if you'd like to," he suggested, peering at her with his piercing, honey-colored eyes.

Even when she wanted to be mad at Maine, she couldn't. *He's so sexy and charming*, she thought. She wanted badly to say, "Go and shower with that bitch you were just texting", but two wrongs don't make a right.

"Sure, bae," she agreed with the fakest smile she could muster up.

Jermaine hopped up like a kid on his way to an amusement park with the biggest grin on his face. He rushed to the bathroom while she discreetly eyed his cheesy ass in disgust. She slowly removed her clothes, increasing her pain with each movement. Lastly she peeled off her panties and bra, tossing them in the laundry basket.

Maine's physique was tantalizing and immaculate. The sight of it alone made Syren's mouth water. His perfectly-trimmed penis hung freely. Boy, did it hang. She climbed in facing him. He spun her around and squeezed her shoulders while placing soft kisses on her neck and collarbone. Her pussy began to drip like a broken faucet and he hadn't even touched it yet.

"I know she wet. Back that ass up so I can see," he whispered in her ear before softly nibbling on her ear obe.

She turned the water off and scooted back, pressing her fat, plush ass against his rock hard penis. He reached his arm around her, spreading her lips with his fingers, sliding them up and down her soaked opening. Soft moans filled the room from the both of them as he played in her juices. He swiftly swiped her clit, forcing her to bite down on her lip. He squatted, using his other hand to spread her butt cheeks, as he entered her from the back. Standing at attention, he eased all nine inches inside her, working and crashing her walls all at once. Using one hand to grip her waist, his other remained on her clit as he pumped himself in and out of her tight love box.

"I'm cumming, Maine," she voiced softly. It was if she lost oxygen with each stroke. Her breathing became irregular and her hands shook uncontrollably as she held onto the railings for dear life.

"That'll be the first of many," he bragged.

And he was correct. She came twice more before he released one, ending the amazing love session Syren loved so much. Her body against the plush mattress felt wonderful. As soon as she positioned her head comfortably against the pillow, she was out - only to be awakened at four in the morning.

"Yes, this is Freelance Security. Is this Syren Wiley?"

"Yes sir," she responded, jumping up in a state of shock.

"According to the screen here, the alarm on window one of the salon just alerted our system here. Two of our men here have been sent. The police were notified first and they're on the way over as well."

"Thank you so much! I'm leaving right now."

Syren noticed Maine's absence from the bed while the security guy was speaking, but she assumed he might have been in the restroom. That was not the case. She cursed underneath her breath while quickly getting dressed. She was moving so fast she forgot to brush her teeth, which she didn't realize until she was reversing out of her driveway. She peered closer into the rearview mirror, wiping the slobber from her cheek and digging the crust from her eyes. Now it was time to check Maine's ass. The phone rang six times before he picked up.

"Jermaine, where are you?"

"Where you think I am, and why are you awake?"

"What do you mean?"

"Well, I left you in bed. I am on my way to your salon, Syren," he admitted, calming her anxiety. She was so sick of Maine and his lies.

"Okay, me too. Bye."

Syren pulled alongside of the curb. From a distance, she could see the shattered glass. She rolled her eyes at the scornful sight.

Who would do something like this? I don't have enemies.

"You're Syren Wiley?" a police officer asked her.

"Yes sir," she responded, looking at the mess.

Some idiot had destroyed the entire front window with a brick. She stepped over the shattered glass into her salon, where she instantly spotted Jermaine speaking with the older officer and the two security guys. Seeing that they had trashed the place too really pissed her off. She buried her face in the palms of her hands as the tears welled in her eyes. It seemed like every time she got ahead, something always pushed her back. Growing up, she never had shit. Maine introduced her to the finer things.

Syren began to think back to a time when she was at the bottom. So far down she couldn't see the path to the top. Before Maine, there was Byron...

***

Greedy Grove, 1998

Syren was just sixteen years of age, dating a guy she had just met and known only a few days. She was naïve as an adolescent and green as pastures, and this particular day, she went to his place with him. To her knowledge, Byron was a drug dealer.

"I want you to stay here with me. I got you," he quoted in between pecks while laying on top of her. "

Byron had made Syren feel so special and complete in the last couple of days they had spent together. "Stay?" she repeated, puzzled.

"Yeah, stay."

"Here with all of your cousins, bae? There's no privacy."

"Bae, if we want privacy, we can get it. I just want you in my presence every waking day and every night before I close my eyes."

His words were like butter to a biscuit. She couldn't do anything but say yes, knowing her mother would lose her cool. But that still didn't change her mind.

"Okay, bae, I will."

He kissed her lips and for the first time, they had sex - sex that Syren thought was mind blowing. She drifted off with a smile on her face, knowing she'd made the right decision, only to be awakened by someone yelling Byron's name. Apparently, the person couldn't wait for him to respond as the guy rushed inside. He didn't look like any of the guys she had seen at the house yesterday when she arrived.

"What's up, Byron?" He glanced at Syren, who in his eyes was asleep.

As Byron turned around, peering up at the man who stood over him, he jumped up. The man eyed Syren lustfully, revealing his crooked smile with an open-faced gold tooth on his left front tooth. It made her feel nervous and uneasy.

"Who's this?" he probed.

"My girl," Byron shot back confidently, yet she could hear the shakiness in his voice.

"You're not going to introduce us?" he asked, squeezing the tip of his dick through his denim jeans.

"Sy-Syren, this is Tyrone. Ty-Tyrone, th-this is Syren," he stammered over his words, obviously afraid.

"Nice to meet you, Ms. Syren." He strolled towards the bed, placing her hand into his and kissing the back of it. His awkward gaze bothered Syren, but she knew not to press the issue if Byron didn't.

"Let me holla at you out here, Byron," Tyrone demanded, making his exit while Byron followed suit.

Syren quickly snatched the sheets off her exposed body and got dressed, dashing to the door and opening it just enough to peek her head out.

"Something happened with the shipment, so things gon' be delayed around here. Shit, everyone will just have to fend for themselves and hold it down until we come up."

"What happened, Rone?" one of the guys said.

"Byron, run to the corner store and get a box of Swishers."

"Okay."

Syren quickly eased the door closed, knowing Byron was on his way back there.

"Bae, I'll be back," he announced, peeking inside.

"Can I go with you?" she asked through pleading eyes.

"Yeah, come on."

They walked through the small and cluttered house. Syren could feel all eyes on her backside as she bypassed the group of men on the way out the door. The sofas were worn out and the house reeked of mothballs and cigarettes. Their conversation ceased when they saw Syren.

"Bae, I don't know if I can do this," she said, stepping off the porch.

"What you mean, Syren?" Byron asked, never slowing his stride. "We thugging, baby," he continued, flashing her a grin. With his smooth caramel-colored skin and both feminine and masculine features, he was the definition of a pretty boy.

"Okay," she agreed.

A few days passed. Although it wasn't the most comfortable setting, Byron's presence and affection alone were enough to help her overlook things she didn't agree with. But the noise, drama, and disrespect towards her and Byron was becoming frustrating.

"Byron, I'm tired of wearing your clothes. Can you just buy me some? If not, I'm going to have to go back home," she voiced in hopes he'd say yes. Honestly, she wasn't welcome home. She hadn't contacted Shelia since the day she made the decision to stay with Byron. She was afraid. She had no clue what exactly she'd be returning to, unsure of how her mother would react.

"Come on, let's go up here to Ross and get you some clothes."

"Hell yeah!" Her eyes lit up at the sound of the discount store. She scurried to her feet and slid her sandals on.

It was scorching hot outside. They made it to the massive store in no time.

"Get what you want, bae," he said, and she did just that. Byron became her own personal cart, holding sandals, underclothes, swimsuits, and outfits.

"Bae, Trae out there in the car waiting on us. Go ahead, I'm coming," he insisted.

"Okay." Syren shrugged, walking out. Once outside, she peered to the left then the right for Trae. There was no sign of his ashy grey Crown Victoria anywhere. She smacked her lips and began to pace the concrete until Trae veered into the lot, driving like a bat out of hell.

The door to Ross flew open. Byron came flying out like a missile, clothes in both hands. The stack of clothes was so high he could barely see past it, nearly knocking over an elderly woman.

"Come on, Syren!" he yelled.

Syren stood there, awestruck and motionless. She couldn't fathom what was occurring.

"Come your crazy ass on, girl!" Trae hollered out the window.

"Syren!"

Apparently, she wasn't moving fast enough. The sound of tires screeching filled the busy lot. All she could see was the smoke coming from the pipe as Trae veered into the busy intersection. The Ross employees rushed out in hopes of finding the shoplifting culprit, Disappointment was written all over their faces once they realized he was gone.

Syren lowered her head in shame and headed back to the "spot", purposely walking at a snail's pace.

"Girl, where you been? You scared me. I was about to come looking for you," Byron spoke, seemingly concerned once he spotted Syren walking up the driveway.

"Yeah, you should've been, since you left me," she mumbled.

"I mean, damn, you want a nigga to get locked up?"

"Why did you steal it?"

"'Why did you steal it?'" he mocked her in a high-pitched tone with an angry scowl plastered across his face. "Look, Syren, I'm tired of pacifying you. Ain't shit sweet around here. I know you can tell I'm just a regular ol' hood nigga. I ain't ballin'. Long as you taken care of, we good. I'm taking risks; not you. Just ride the wave, man. As long as you remain above water, you good."

"You right, bae. I don't want to argue."

"Come on," he said, draping his arm over her shoulder, guiding her inside.

"Bae, watch out, I have to pee," she whispered, running to the restroom.

"Hold on!" he shouted, but she paid him no mind.

A sigh of relief escaped her lips as she sat on the toilet, releasing the bladder she had held for hours. She wiped and flushed, but the toilet didn't make a move. She pushed the handle down a second time, but nothing. She wiggled it to the left then to the right, yet still nothing

"Byron!" she called out.

"I tried to tell you, the water is off. Here, take this," he said, handing her a yellow bucket full of water.

"What's that supposed to do?"

"Watch out," he demanded, pouring the water into the toilet.

She watched him, ashamed. She was embarrassed of the situation and for Byron. He went out of his way to impress Syren, yet this wasn't impressive by far. Like magic, the yellow toilet water turned clear and the tissue vanished.

"I'm sorry," Syren apologized for no particular reason.

"It's okay, mama," he replied with a half-smile while matching her gaze. He grabbed her hand and said, "Syren, you're going to have to get with the program."

"Okay," she agreed. "How will I bathe?"

"The neighbors are letting us use their water hose, so I'm going to fill the bucket up until the tub is full."

Syren stared at Byron in agreement, but on the inside, she was going nuts.

Nearly an hour later, Byron was finished filling the tub. She removed her clothes and stepped in. The feeling of the lukewarm water angered her, but she made the best of it. Feeling refreshed and rejuvenated, she threw on the pajama set she'd gotten from Ross and lay next to Byron on the air mattress.

"This thing is deflating, Byron."

"No it's not. You tripping."

"Okay," she responded, not wanting to argue. Moments later, they were on the floor.

"Damn, bae, you was right. Move out the way so I can air it up," he said, grabbing the small machine that sat in the corner of the room. Just as he was about to plug in the machine, the 20" TV went black.

"What the fuck?" Syren whispered. Her scowl was evident that she was not only confused, but shocked as well.

Byron went to press the power button on the TV, but nothing happened.

"They turned the electricity off. You need a candle, fam? I have an extra one!"

"That's it! Uh-uh, Byron! I love you, but I have to go."

Syren jumped to her feet. She quickly got dressed and walked next door to the neighbor's house. Byron tried stopping her, but it was useless. Her mind was made up. Syren phoned her mother, making up some dramatic story about being kidnapped. Ms Sheila was parked outside Byron's neighbor's house within five minutes. Within that time, she went and said her goodbyes.

"I love you, Byron. I'll keep in touch. Once we both mature and grow financially and mentally, then we can give this thing called us another shot." She really did love Byron, but she could no longer live under such conditions.

"A'ight, boo," he responded, looking away before the tears in his eyes fell onto his cheek.

She stood along the curb next door then climbed into her mother's hoopty once she arrived, never looking back.

Three months later, Syren found out that Byron was sentenced to fifteen years in prison for possession of meth and unlawfully carrying an illegal firearm. He was so eager to become a drug dealer that he moved too fast for his own good. A little after she met Maine, she was still sending Byron letters and money sporadically, but after having Jaelyn, she completely stopped. She hadn't heard from or seen Byron since then.

Chapter 4
Long day of work

"Thanks, baby," Syren whispered, kissing her fiancé on the lips.

Maine peered down, admiring her beauty. Her bronze skin and 5'4" curvy frame were stunning. She had ass and thighs for days. The weekly trips to Pappadeaux added a little fat around her abdominal area. It wasn't hanging over her jeans or anything. It was just a small pudge that Maine actually found attractive. Her juicy lips shone from the lip gloss she had recently applied.

"You welcome, mama," he whispered in her ear, wrapping his arm around her frame. He peered at Uh'Nija's salty ass. Pursed lips and her brows nearly touching…there was no denying that she was mad as hell.

"I'll see you at the crib. I'm about to link up with Dekari," he mentioned, taking a step back.

"Okay," Syren agreed cheerfully.

He pinched her butt before walking out, giving Uh'Nija one last glance over his shoulders. The smirk on her face was mischievous and devious. *If she plotting, she better plan her burial while she at it, 'cause I'll kill a bitch before I let her come in between me and my home,* Maine thought as he made his way to his office.

"What's up, boy?" Dekari greeted him when he arrived, sitting at the table in his office.

"What's up? I'm glad you here. We have to go put this eviction notice on 214," he continued.

"Bet, and I appreciate you for coming through last night."

"You know I got you. That wasn't shit."

Dekari and Maine left the office and made their way to apartment 214. The Falls wasn't as hood as the projects, but they were a little ratchet. Kids ran around on the pavement barefoot. The ones a little older fucked, smoked weed, and shot dice. They didn't think Maine knew they jumped the gate and snuck in the pool around midnight.

"Excuse me, sir!" a lady yelled from behind.

"Don't look back," Maine whispered to Dekari.

"Sir! Sir!"

"What?" they both yelled in unison, turning around at the same time.

"Look, I'm sorry to bother you, but this the third time this week that I've found this little nappy neck boy in my house fooling with my daughter."

They felt sorry for the unusually thin elderly woman, who looked to be suffering from Parkinson's. Eager to hear more and shocked as well, Maine asked, "Fooling with your daughter how?"

"They in the damn room having sex."

"Oh, I'm sorry, ma'am but——"

"Ma'am, that's on you. Whoop that fast-ass daughter of yours!" Maine interjected, cutting Dekari short.

"Fuck both of y'all black asses!" she hollered at the two of them.

They walked away, laughing. They hated when they had to leave the office. Tenants stopped and harassed them like they were celebrities. Ninety percent of their problems were much greater than what they could handle.

As they stood in front 214, Maine peered around the window, squinting to see past the blinds, but it was useless.

"It's no one in there. Fuck it, let's go."

As soon as Dekari and Maine proceeded to walk away, the sound of locks clicking caught both of their attention. They looked in the direction of the sudden noise, waiting to see whoever was on the other side of the door.

Two guys emerged. One guy was zipping his pants up while the other guy peered around skeptically.

"Hey, y'all see that notice?" Maine asked, peering at them both in disgust.

"We don't live here. A friend of ours do and allowed us to rent the spot for a few hours," he revealed, grinning at Dekari.

"Say, bitch-ass nigga, I don't play them type of games. You betta get yo' gay ass on before I knock yo' bitch ass out!"

Maine chuckled at Dekari's threat.

The other guy never slowed his stride. He didn't want his cover blown. He actually looked familiar to Maine, but he didn't attempt to rack his brain. His profession required him to meet a thousand people.

"Okay, boo, whatever," he voiced, locking the door before strutting off. Dude was masculine as hell with a high-pitched voice. His hands were twice the size of Maine's with an excessive amount of ash on his knuckles. He was black as motor oil with lips the color of the opening inside of a vagina. A loop earring hung from his left ear. His shoulders were broad and his frame began to narrow at his waist, making his figure resemble a Dorito chip. He wore a tight Abercrombie shirt with ripped blue jeans and a pair of Old Navy flip flops

"Come on. We'll come back later to see if she's here," Maine told Dekari, patting him on the back.

The punk had Dekari so upset that he still stood in the same spot.

Dra'Neisha Collins was the name of the tenant they were hunting for. She had been a resident for only nine months and had three months left on her lease. Maine said her name repeatedly in his mind, but he couldn't put a face with name. Since that apartment wasn't in view of the office, he never saw who left or came.

"You holler at them shorties yet?"

"Which ones?" Dekari asked, closing the door to the office once they made it inside.

"The strippers, Black and Yellow."

"Oh nah, not yet."

"What's the hold up?" Maine questioned.

"What's the rush?"

"Ain't no pressure on no bitch, dawg."

"I can't tell. I don't even know why you so pressed. You laid up in some different pussy damn near every night."

"You sound like you mad. You the single one. You can be climbing in some pussy every night rightfully!" Maine clapped back, leaning up.

"Don't worry 'bout me. I'm not mad, but Maine, you need to start being smarter with the shit. Them bullshit-ass stunts you be pulling ain't gon' work one day and you gon' end up losing Syren, man."

"You right, man," he agreed, letting out a deep breath.

"Excuse me," a dreadhead announced, peeking inside the office.

"What's up?" Dekari called out, throwing his hands up.

"I'm Dra'Neisha Collins. I stay in apartment——"

"Dra'Neisha?" Dekari and Maine blurted out in shock.

"Yes, Dra'Neisha Collins, apartment 214."

"Come in. Damn, I thought you were—— That doesn't even matter. Come on," Dekari spoke as he waved her inside. He began to pry into her personal life.

Maine sat at his desk emotionless, not moved or interested in the woman who portrayed herself to be a man. She was actually quite attractive. He watched her and Dekari go back and forth like they'd known each other forever. Maine shook his head at Dra'Neisha in disgust. She wore a crisp white Burberry shirt, khaki cargo shorts, matching bucket hat, and a pair of Air Force Ones - all white, to be exact.

Maine felt repugnance for gays. He couldn't stand the fact that they changed their appearances to become something they weren't. If Jaelyn ever decided that he was suddenly curious and wanted to be a little girl, he would dispose of his ass like Lucious did Jamal Lyon on the TV show *Empire*.

"Something came up, but if you could just give me a few hours, I'll have the money," she reasoned.

"Why, so you can rent it out again? You're violating your contract, bruh. I don't run a brothel. I run a business!" he shot back, reclined in his leather chair.

"I understand, Mister…?" She paused, awaiting Maine's response.

"Bossman," Maine replied, grinning arrogantly.

"Mr. Bossman, I didn't mean no disrespect. I apologize. But if you're willing to wait, I'll be parked outside first thing in the morning with your money."

"There's no need for all that. You have two hours, chick. Here's my card so you can reach me."

"Thank you, sir," she spoke gratefully and mannerably, placing the card in her pocket before walking out.

Dekari eyed Maine from across the room in disbelief.

"What?" he asked, pretending to be lost.

"Nothing, man," Dekari replied, shaking his head.

The sound of Dekari's text message alert rang out.

"The sisters on their way."

***

"Damn, you not gon' take nothing off? You just going to continue and dance fully dressed?" Maine asked, eyeing the dark-skinned sister, then glancing over to Dekari.

"He's right. What's up? Gotdamn!"

65

"Well, y'all niggas ain't throwing no money," the light-skinned sister voiced, twirling her curls with her fingers. She was referred to as "Yella".

"Gotdamn, we giving y'all a pass on this month's rent," Maine argued.

"Yeah, but——'"

"But what? Alright man. Y'all black bitches so ungrateful," Maine said, pulling the small wad of large bills from his pocket. He never kept a large sum of money on him because there wasn't anything pleasant about the Grove, but today he planned on shopping for Syren and Jaelyn once he clocked out of the office. "Come on."

Both of their eyes lit up like a full moon once the two men retrieved the money.

"Bands will make you dance huh?" Dekari asked, thumbing through the stack of money, grinning mischievously.

Black, which was the darker sister, strutted towards her phone that was plugged into the speakers, changing the tune. Da Baby's song "Vibes" played loudly through the small speaker. Yella stood off to the side while Black hit the pole first. She climbed all the way to the top and slid down with her legs outstretched. The monster inside Maine's pants twitched as he peered up at her fat print through her red lace thong. She slid down, landing into a Chinese split, bouncing up and down like hydraulics. Since all Maine had was twenties, he threw two on the floor near her and slid one inside her bra strap discreetly, trying to break the clamp that held it together. Unable to do so, he smoothly eased back down into the leather chair. She slowly crawled towards the two money-throwing men. She resembled a dark-skinned version of Pocahontas. Her hair was long and straight. Perhaps they may have been contacts, but her eyes were grey.

She sexy as hell, Dekari thought.

Black rose up on her knees, watching the men closely while unclamping and removing her bra. The longer she took, the more eager they became. They stared down at the chick they called Black, stunned and confused.

"What the fuck?" Dekari blurted.

Everything seemed to have stopped. Black stopped moving. Yella stopped swaying her hips and snapping her fingers in the corner. Although the music still played, you would've thought that had stopped too.

"What?" Black asked, looking dumbfounded.

"Oh, so you don't see the problem?" Dekari asked with his mouth twisted to the side.

"Ugh, no," she replied, throwing her hair over her shoulder.

"So you don't—— What's wrong with the left one?" Maine asked, cutting to the chase, pointing at her saggy left breast.

"Oh, this?" She chuckled, waving it off. "One of my implants fell. I have to get it fixed," she explained. Her left breast sagged nearly to the center of her stomach, whereas the right one resembled a doorknob.

"Bruh, you don't work at Onyx like that. Not the Onyx," Maine spoke, shaking his head. Totally vexed and disturbed, he stood to his feet. "Look, come back when all ya ducks in a row," Maine continued, stopping the music

"Wait! What about me? I'm good. Everything sitting pretty! Let me make my bread," Yella reasoned, removing her shirt.

"We'll check you out tomorrow. I'm not even feeling this shit no more. Just go.

Bzzz! Bzzz!

Maine lifted his finger to his mouth before answering the phone. "Hey Ma."

"Go get your sister before they hide her ass under the jail.
She down there selling that shit!"

"She what?"

"You heard what I said!"

"Okay, okay, I'm on my way."

Click!

"Get dressed. I got business to tend to," Maine announced,
putting things back in order.

"Who was that?"

"My momma. They just kicked Bre'untae's ass out of
school."

"What her li'l ass done did now?"

"I don't know. I'm about to see. I'll see you in the
morning. Be easy," Maine told Dekari before walking out of
the office.

He was parked right outside the office. He hopped in his
2014 Camaro and peeled off. He wasted no time getting Syren
on the line. "Bae, I'll be home later. I'm on my way to Navarro
College."

"You what? For what?"

"Bre'untae got caught selling drugs on campus. They
kicking her out. "

"Okay, come get me from the shop. I'm going too."

"Fine, Syren, if you want to come, be ready." He couldn't
blame her ass. If he was her, he wouldn't believe him either.
Maine was just an addict, but drugs, alcohol, and guns weren't
his addiction. Pussy was his problem. He was a sex addict.
Counseling didn't even help.

Maine honked the horn when he got outside the salon.

Syren strutted out of the salon with her Balenciaga bag on
her arm. She walked with a purpose, as if she was a detective
who had just cracked a case. She always thought she was two
steps ahead.

Syren activated the alarm on her Dodge Challenger before climbing inside of Maine's Camaro.

"You leaving your car?"

"I'll get it on the way back. The girls will keep an eye on it. The shop don't close til 7 p.m. Five hours is enough time to get there and back."

Ah'Million

Chapter 5
The choice is yours

"Maybe they'll let you return next semester," Rashad mentioned, helping Tae pack her belongings.

"Man, it's a wrap. They not hearing shit. Not only am I banned from here, it's going to be tough enrolling someplace else."

"Can't give up. Whatever you do, don't stop trying."

Family and friends referred to Bre'untae as Tae. The last thing she expected was this. This year was her third year in college and since enrolling, she had things on lock, from kush to lean and pills. Everyone who resided in the small town knew it as well.

Tae originally began hustling when her girlfriend Iesha was arrested for fraud a year after they started dating. Tae had a sense of guilt and obligation since it was Tae's idea. She made a vow to herself that she would stand behind Iesha her entire bid if she had to. Iesha was her down chick. They began dating in high school and attended the same college up until Iesha was sent to the Feds. Even though she still had eighty-five percent of her eight year sentence to complete, it still didn't alter her feelings or commitment. Tae's main focus since then had been simple: chasing the bag, finishing school, and holding it down for Iesha.

"Real bitches do real shit – one," she quoted, slowly descending the steps.

Tae quickly blinked away the tears that welled in her eyes, afraid Maine would see them. She was so upset with herself for fucking up at the finish line. Tae had one year left of college to receive her Bachelor's in Environmental Science. As adolescents, her mother had always shown more interest in Maine, crediting and appraising him for every single accomplishment and making excuses on his behalf when he failed. Tae wanted more than anything to outdo her brother just to hear a "good job" or "well done" from her apathetic mother.

***

"Where is she?" Maine mumbled, slowly peering around.

"I don't see Tae; just that he/she right there." Syren pointed.

"Who?"

"That stud broad."

"Hold on, let me ask her if she knows Bre'untae," he said, letting the windows down, hanging out the window. "Aye, hey, excuse me——"

"Who you talking to?" Bre'untae stopped walking and peered around, dumbfounded.

"Tae?" Maine asked, peering through squinted eyes.

"Yeah, baby, it's me."

"Bre'untae?" Syren said, appalled.

"What's up, fam?" She grinned.

Syren glanced up at Tae, completely taken aback as she stood outside the car.

"Damn, y'all gon' open the door?" she asked with both hands full.

Syren was so stunned she forgot the task at hand. She swiftly pressed the unlock button while studying Tae's new look. She had definitely altered her entire appearance since the last time, even her walk. No strut, no twist, just a masculine limp.

Since Syren could remember, Tae had always had flawless skin, which magnified her neatly trimmed edge up. Her plaits were a bit scraggy, giving her a rugged look. She had tattoos all over her brown skin, from her neck to her ankles. The diamond in her ear wasn't massive, but it wasn't small either. It glistened smoothly. Her eyes were the color of peanut butter, but her deep dimples were her biggest charm.

"Bruh, when did this happen?" Maine asked, stunned, eyeing her from head to toe. Although her new look wasn't at all appealing to him, she rocked the hell out of the Fila get-up.

"What's up? Bruh, I got tired of all the feminine shit. I'm not trying to be something I'm not. I'm just comfortable. This look fits my attitude. I'm thuggin'."

"Thuggin'?" Maine repeated with his brow raised.

"Yeah. Fuck all of that. I missed you." She grinned.

"I miss you too. You remember Syren, huh? I know it's been a minute, but not that long."

"Yeah," Tae responded dryly.

The smoke faded as soon as Maine mentioned her name. Tae had never really been fond of Syren and she made it plain and clear that she was just another one of Maine's typical chicks. Syren usually went out of her way doing things to appease Tae, but she refused to do so this time.

Maine must've picked up on the tension as he side eyed Tae discreetly before diverting the conversation.

"Are you going to look for another school? Perhaps a community college?"

"For right now, I think I'm going to take a little break," Tae made known while stuffing her belongings into the backseat.

"So what exactly happened? Momma called me being dramatic."

"I'll tell you when we land," Tae responded, peering through the rearview mirror.

Syren shortly met her gaze. *Whether she tells him now or later, he still going to tell me,* she thought. Syren's left brow raised as she smirked with confidence.

"Cool," Maine responded with a shrug of his shoulders before peeling out.

***

"Call me as soon as you make it home!" Maine leaned over and hollered out of the passenger window from the driver's seat.

"Okay. I'm just making sure everything is locked up and then I'm leaving!" Syren yelled back before rushing inside the salon. She was quite sure everything was in order, but since the window incident, she'd been extra cautious. She opened the door, feeling around the usual spot for the light switch.

"Gotcha!" She flicked on the light switch, immediately spotting Kreesha's big ass on the countertop in front of one of the six large mirrors getting her pussy eaten. They were so in tune with each other neither of them noticed the bright lights or the figure standing before them.

"Kreesha!" Syren yelled, startling Kreesha.

Chris paid her no mind. His head remained buried in between Kreesha's huge thighs. Kreesha peered directly into her eyes as she mouthed the words, "I'm sorry." She continued rolling and bucking her hips while biting down on her lip, making unmanageable and unattractive sex faces. Her eyes rolled to the back of her head, then a loud outburst fell from her lips.

"Disrespectful!" Syren voiced to no one in particular at the despicable sight. "Kreesha!"

"Huh?" she slurred breathlessly with one eye open. She looked groggy and drained.

"Make sure my shit locked up," Syren said, flicking the light switch off before walking out.

Syren sped away from the salon fuming. She drove like a bat out of hell and every time the wind slammed against her face, her spirit softened. She squirmed uncontrollably in the driver's seat of her Challenger while pondering deeply on the disgusting scene she had just witnessed. She hopped out, wasting no time unlocking the front door. She dashed to the restroom to relieve herself, loosening the button on her tight jeans. In a matter of seconds, she was yanking her jeans down. She flopped down on the toilet seat, prepping for the sweet relief. She closed her eyes as the urine oozed from her urethra. An unpleasant feeling compelled her to tighten every lower muscle she had.

"Sssss," she hissed, wincing at the pain, which was unbearable and made her so miserable she regretted pissing all together. "What the fuck?" she whispered, hesitating to urinate. Slowly she relieved herself as smoothly as possible, but it still wasn't anything close to smooth. "Hell nawl!" she voiced loudly, pulling up her jeans.

Jermaine had fucked up for the last time.

***

Kreesha couldn't believe Syren had caught her fucking in the salon.

"You too old for your pussy to be that hot," Uh'Nija commented while plucking her eyebrows.

Kreesha lay out on the couch beside Uh'Nija, who was seated on the floor peering into the small shaving mirror. They both resided in the same apartment complex under Maine and Dekari' smanagement. That was beneficial on Kreesha's behalf since she had a form of relation to the owner.

De'erick and Meagan, her teenage kids, made things quite difficult financially. They were at the age where swag wasn't an option; it was required. Meagan had recently become a cheerleader. In addition to the cost associated with that, her school things were very expensive. Everything now was just a big competition. Now that she was just entering high school, Meagan was going to get everything she desired. Luckily, Maine would give her passes if her rent was late. For the most part, she had ways to pay her rent if her funds were scanty.

Uh'Nija, on the other hand, had no problem popping pussy for a nigga. She knew Maine had a family and that he would not ever be hers once the night ended, but that still didn't stop her. She got a thrill out of it all. Materialistically, she wanted for nothing.

"I know, girl, I just couldn't control myself. He brought me some Panda Express, and while I was eating, he began to sex me with those eyes. I tried ignoring him, but it only made him get physical, and once he started using hands, I set the Chinese food down and it happened," she explained, shrugging her shoulders.

"So what exactly did your cousin see?"

"My big ass on the counter with his head buried in between my legs."

"Whose counter were you on?"

"Yours, bitch!" Kreesha retorted.

"Ugh, nasty ass! You better have bleached my shit!" she yelled, throwing her slipper at Kreesha with the most disgusted scowl she could muster. "I would've fired your ass," she continued, standing to her feet with her hand resting on her hip.

"One of your dude's mothers walked in on your slut ass in her bed, so the audacity of you to look down on me!" Kreesha shot back.

Uh'Nija sauntered off towards the rear of the apartment.

The sound of the ringing phone diverted Kreesha's attention. Being the nosy bitch she was, she hopped up and ran over to the kitchen counter where Uh'Nija's phone was sitting. Swiftly and quietly she checked the message, which was irrelevant, then continued to scroll through her inbox.

It was quite difficult since the majority of her messages were from unknown contacts, so Kreesha had to open each message from every random number. Something she peeped had been hounding her spirit and she was desperate to get to the bottom of it. Most of the texts were from random men. The disapproving scowl was evidence that Kreesha was displeased with Uh'Nija's lifestyle.

"Bingo," she whispered, scrolling down the message history. Although the message was three days old, it was new to her.

817-555-6231: Quit texting my phone
Uh'Nija: I'm sorry baby.

All the texts that were exchanged between the two surfaced, taking Kreesha by surprise.

The sound of the toilet flushing caused her to jump in fear. She placed the phone back down, praying the screen light would grow dim before Uh'Nija returned and noticed. As soon as Kreesha's backside hit the cushion, Uh'Nija emerged from the back. She took longer than usual, which was a good thing.

"Uh'Nija!" she yelled, trying to keep her from noticing the lit screen. She scowled at Kreesha, evidently perplexed, but softened once Kreesha asked, "Hey what color dress would look good on Meagan for prom?"

"Um, me personally, I would go with a soft purple," she voiced confidently.

Kreesha looked past her, seeing that the screen was no longer lit. She rose to her feet and gathered her things. She had one focus and one focus only.

"Okay, I'm going to keep that in mind. Now I'm going to see if these kids where they supposed to be."

"Alright, be careful, and call me when you make it inside."

Kreesha almost fell trying to get to her apartment. Avoiding the group of guys that hung out on the stoop, she continued to move until she got to her destination. A smile slowly covered her face as she spotted the man she had been looking for.

"What's up, Kreesha?" A hint of curiosity danced behind his honey-colored eyes after he noticed the smirk on her face.

"What's up, playboy?" she responded, grinning.

"I've been looking for you. You know Meagan's prom is coming up——"

"Look, Kreesha," he intervened, cutting her short. "You've been late for the past three months. I can't afford to give you any more extensions. Tell ol' boy whose head you was riding in my wife's shop about what's occurring in your life. I've heard enough. I need my money, man," he expressed.

"While I'm telling her my problems, would you like for me to tell her about you and Uh'Nija while I'm at it?" she asked, forcing Maine to stop dead in his tracks

"What you say?" he questioned through narrowly slitted eyes.

"I didn't stutter! Tell her about Uh'Nija! Co-worker! Friend! Employee! Nigga, should I keep going?"

"She's not going to believe it 'cause you don't even believe that yourself. Uh'Nija, out of all people? What's so special about her?"

"These text messages I screenshotted and sent to my phone, that's what so special. Quit playing with me. That's my motherfucking cousin, Maine!"

"What is it you want, Kreesha?" he asked in a low tone. His shoulders sagged in defeat. Without meeting her gaze, his eyes remained trained on the pavement.

"I'm not going to tax you. I know you a dirty dick-ass nigga. My cousin dumb enough to stick around, fine by me."

"You ho's kill me with that shit. If you was my bitch, you'd deal with it too. Quit speaking on the 'what if's'; until or unless you're in those shoes, 'cause you ain't too good to fall. It's a pattern, and your fat ass will fall in line too."

"So you mad?"

"Nah, you always in my business, but the truth out. Just make your request known so I can go on my way. "

"I just want a three month pass on rent every——"

"Say no more," Maine rudely chimed in, slightly brushing her arm as he bypassed her.

Bzzz! Bzzz! Bzzz! Kreesha peered down to her phone to read the text message.

Syren: I have a doctor's appointment in the a.m. need u 2 open
Kreesha: Ok

Ah'Million

Chapter 6
Once a fool, always a fool

Uh'Nija turned the volume up on her phone as she listened to the music on Sound cloud through her Airpods. This was Uh'Nija's way of drowning out the cries from the adolescents that accompanied their mothers. Only an hour had passed, yet she was already exhausted. She was so distraught that she and Maine hadn't spoke so she called Syren and lied and cried to her for an hour, hoping she'd hear his voice in the background, but it never happened.

The lobby resembled the food stamp office. Infants of different races crawled and ran freely through the aisles. The paint on the chairs had begun to peel. Tiny graffiti decorated the walls, but she had seen worse.

"Ms. Marshall!" the nurse yelled.

Uh'Nija rushed to respond. She entered the stall and filled the cup. Uh'Nija was fuming on the inside. Here she was with an ill pussy and on the other hand, Syrenn was still roaming around with the man Uh'Nija would die for.

"Give me five minutes," the nurse said, walking out of the room.

Uh'Nija was ninety-nine percent sure it was chlamydia. The symptoms were familiar. She peered straight ahead, recalling her past visits to the clinic. She was always alone to face her fears. Her cousin accompanied her once when she had gotten pregnant, only to have a miscarriage shortly after.

Uh'Nija barely had any friends growing up, especially during her teen years. The few she did accumulate were because her mother, who was a single parent, worked a lot, leaving their home vacant. That permitted her and her "friends" to do as they pleased. Other friends she couldn't keep because she flirted or blatantly fucked their lovers. Her mother's male friends were no exception either. She was outright ratchet. By the grace of God, she never had a deadly or incurable disease.

"Ms. Marshall, according to the test, you're negative for all the STD's with the exception of chlamydia. Your pregnancy results came back negative as well. Per protocol, I have to ask this question. It's imperative you answer honestly."

"Yes ma'am."

"What's the name of the partner you had sex with last?"

Uh'Nija considered lying, but changed her mind. Lie or truth, it was harmless.

"Jermaine Wiley."

The doctor squinted at Uh'Nija inquisitively, making her regret mentioning Jermaine's name at that instant.

"Okay, I'm writing this prescription. Pay for it and pick it up at the counter on your way out. Take one a day for seven days and you'll be cured. No sex for seven days, or it will harm the process."

"Thank you, Dr. Samuels," she said before leaving. She stopped by the prescription counter, to pick up her medicine before proceeding out the front door.

The feeling of shame and paranoia no longer surfaced after leaving the clinic. She had become a regular. The first few times she would disguise herself just to go unnoticed, but her perspective had really changed since then. She hated how reckless she was with her pussy. Her aunt used to tell her all the time, "Uh'Nija, be careful, babygirl, you only get one," pointing at the body part between her legs.

But the raw flesh drilling her walls and the thrill of the possibility that things could go wrong excited Uh'Nija more than anything.

She parked along the side of the curb in front of the salon. She only had two appointments today and after that, she was leaving. She pondered being a little messy and mischievious, but the last thing she wanted was to lose Maine.

"Bitch, where you been? I called you," Kreesha voiced loudly as soon as she set her purse in her booth.

If it was anyone other than Kreesha, Uh'Nija probably would've gave attitude, but you had to just love Kreesha's free spirit.

"I was at the clinic," Uh'Nija whispered. Her eyes scurried swiftly, making sure no one heard her. The salon wasn't packed, but it was far from empty and too full of ho's from the hood. Tonight the Dallas Mavericks and the Milwaukee Bucks played, so everyone who was someone or thought they were someone would be in attendance.

"Bitch, for what?" she asked in a low tone, looking appalled. Kreesha was so dramatic.

"S -T-D," Uh'Nija signed with her fingers.

"Do it again," Kreesha whispered.

Uh'Nija smacked her lips, then did it again.

"STD?"

"Yes."

"Damn, bitch, you know them niggas stay dirty dick dancing. I don't know why you don't make them strap up."

"I know, friend. I'm so embarrassed. "

"Don't be. Syren left five minutes before you did."

"Yeah, but Syren is probably pregnant," she said before sighing deeply.

"If you call that something looming inside of her 'chlamydia'."

Her heart smiled when Kreesha revealed the news. *Little Ms. Perfect has an STD*, she thought, smirking devilishly.

"Come on, Rita!" she called out to one of her customers, who had come in while she was conversing with Kreesha.

***

Maine sat in his office, pondering hiring a hitman for Kreesha's big ass. He had enough of her ass messing with his business. Then again, he had to count his blessings because she could've easily run and told Syren everything. Surprisingly, she didn't. That almighty dollar would make you sin and turn on family and friends. With the solid information she claimed to have, he just knew she would request more than that. He would've given her a blank check and told her to insert the amount desired. Inwardly, he was glad when she settled for the petty request.

"Susan, pack up. I found someone to replace you."

Susan sat frozen at her desk, peering up at Maine in disbelief.

"Bruh, I told you I don't want to be no apartment clerk. I'm going to get me one of those booths at Lil Ced's barber shop down the street," Tae intervened.

"Okay, Susan, never mind. You're still employed."

Dekari chuckled lightly. If looks could kill, Maine would be on the cold steel with the yellow tag attached to his toe.

"If that's the case, you can cop a booth at Syren's salon. You're guaranteed to come up. You'll be the only barber."

"I don't know, man, I'll think about it. I never could vibe with ya girl."

"Sis, you never liked Syren."

"She just sneaky to me. There was something she did in particular to give me a reason to think that way but I just can't remember," Tae said, biting her bottom lip, fondling the imaginary hair on her chin.

She appeared to be in deep thought, so Maine remained quiet. Honestly, he wanted to hear what she had to say.

"I truly believe her, and——"

"Hey, there's Uh'Nija," Dekari announced.

"Uh'Nija?" Tae repeated.

Maine had invited Uh'Nija over when he received her text. After all the drama, she was still looking out for his best interests at heart.

"Tell her to come to the back," Maine voiced, heading in that direction.

"Close the door," he ordered/ His dick twitched instantly as soon as their eyes met. He didn't understand what it was about Uh'Nija that he was so attracted to. Whatever it was, it was dangerous. The fresh pixie cut gave her an exotic spin. Her bright eyeshadow was a bit extreme, but it gave her a sexy finish. The polish on her nails matched her toes and the colored diamond on her nose ring. The Puma T-shirt and extremely short spandex shorts hugged her figure to perfection, revealing the artwork on her thighs and calves.

"Sit down."

"I'd rather stand," she shot back, surprising him with her evasiveness.

"I got your text. I need you to go to the clinic, tell your doctor you misplaced your prescription and you need to purchase another one."

"I can do that," she agreed, massaging her fingers through her hair.

Unconsciously staring at her from head to toe, he forgot the task at hand. He eased out of his chair and walked slowly towards her. He could sense the panic since she avoided eye contact. He grazed his nose across the back of her neck, inching closer behind her. His penis was now extended, poking her left butt cheek. The simple and smooth gesture made Uh'Nija bite down on her bottom lip.He swiftly grabbed her hands, which were at her side to limit her movement. The last thing he wanted was for her to resist. It had been three days since he touched, felt and stroked her insides.

"Stop," she protested, forcefully jerking away.

"I don't want a quickie. I want all of you. I'll see you tonight," he stated.

I guess we can fuck once more before we begin this seven day fast, she thought as she walked out of the office.

He hung back in the office, waiting for his dick to go limp.

"Hey, you have everything together? I'm going to the mall to cop me something for the game tonight."

"Yeah, we good. Me and Susan going to leave an hour early. Meet me at my place. We gon' all ride out together."

"Bet."

"Alright, y'all, be safe!" Dekari yelled, walking out of the door.

"Bruh, what game y'all going to see?" Tae asked.

"Dallas plays the Milwaukee Bucks."

"Oh, okay."

"You want to go?"

"Maybe."

Chapter 7
Nothing is promised or guaranteed

"Don't forget to send me that book. My celly acting funny with her copy," Iesha spoke into the receiver.

"I got you, mama, and I'll add more funds to your commissary."

"Thank you, baby."

"You have one minute left," the automated system announced.

Iesha smacked her lips, something she did every call after hearing that.

"It's almost over. I promise to be here with you and for you for the rest of your stay. You have more time behind you than you do in front of you. I love you. Call me when you wake up," Tae said in hopes of lifting her spirit.

"Okay. I love you."

Click.

"Aunty Tae, why you look like a boy?" Jaelyn asked as soon as Tae slid her phone in her pocket.

She chuckled at Jaelyn's comment before responding. "Nephew, I'm just thugging. I still and always will be Aunty Tae."

"Tae, could you text or call Maine and see if he's on his way?" Syren asked.

"That's yo' nigga. Why can't you do it?"

"I've been trying," she pleaded.

Tae dialed her mother's number, purposely ignoring her. She waited patiently for her mother to answer.

"Hey Momma."

"Hello, Bre'untae."

"Can I stop by to see you in the morning?"

"Like I told you a few days ago, I raised a man and a woman, not two men. Until you change your appearance, you're not welcome in my house. In my house, we will serve the Lord!"

Click.

Tae had been trying to sway her mother into allowing her to come home since she had been kicked out of school. It had been two years since she had seen her, but after the day she arrived and her mother caught a glimpse of her, she hadn't seen her since. Honestly, she was done trying. That was who she had become and her mother needed to accept it. She was not a child anymore and at this point in her life, she was free to do whatever she pleased. Tae didn't understand why her mother would disown her just because she switched her swag up.

Tae slid the phone into her black Fendi jeans and headed to the front room. Since she wasn't allowed in her mother's home, Maine and Syren allowed her to stay with them in their five bedroom home.

Iesha had been Tae's boo for years. She was her everything. They had that Lauren London and T.I. from the movie *A.T.L.* kind of love. Although they were both from different walks of life, they both had dreams and goals they were hoping to achieve. Things got a little difficult then Tae swayed her to join her in a scheme she'd forever regret, which cost Iesha more than she expected. Iesha and Tae hooked up when she was still Bre'untae. She didn't judge her for her sudden desire to alter her appearance. She even ignored the false rumors about Tae using her for her money. Iesha's finances came from her parents, but after finding out about Tae, they cut her off financially, agreeing to pay for her classes only. That's why Tae started selling drugs on and off campus. But like they say, you can never have enough. The more you get, the more you want. She didn't want to appear less of a mate, so she did what she felt was best. However, what's best isn't always what's right.

"What's up, y'all?" Dekari announced, walking into the living room.

Syren followed close behind. His cologne spread throughout the room like an airborne disease. He was dressed in a Balmain sweatsuit and a pair of all white Air Force Ones.

"What's up, De?"

"Uncle De!" Jaelyn yelled, throwing his hands in the air.

"I see ya," he complimented as Jaelyn slowly spun around, showing off his Giannis jersey.

"I got a seamstress that can alter that jersey a little bit." Dekari spoke in a low tone to Syren about Jaelyn's one size too big jersey. "Y'all ready?" he asked, peering at the three of them.

"We waiting on Maine," Tae responded.

"Let me call to see if he's on the way," he voiced, walking out.

Tae was convinced Dekari was truly concerned and in doubt of Maine's absence until she noticed his nose flare and his eyes roll once he bypassed Jaelyn on the way out. The look spoke volumes and it told her he wasn't surprised or baffled by Maine's inability to be present. Tae glanced over at a distressed Syren, who tried disguising her anguish with a tight-lipped smile.

"Hey, he's not picking up," Dekari confirmed, searching everyone's eyes - especially Jaelyn's.

"Fuck it - I mean, forget it – let's go without him," Tae said.

"Yeah we can't let these tickets go to waste, and besides, me and Jaelyn been planning this for months. Ain't that right, li'l man?"

"Yep! I'm ready to go, Uncle De."

"Tae, you can get Maine's ticket."

"Okay."

"Wait, I forgot, I gave Maine his ticket to him at the office."

"It's okay. Tae, take mine. Enjoy yourselves. I'm tired and I need to catch up on my sleep anyways," Syren said, forcing herself to yawn.

"Bye, Mama," Jaelyn said, heading for the door.

"You sure, Syren? We can just buy one," Dekari added.

"I'm positive. Thanks for coming. Jaelyn has been talking about this game for weeks. I just wish it was just as important to Maine like it is to you," she said, smiling coyly.

Tae didn't comment. Although there were things she did disagree with, she wouldn't dare discuss those things with Syren. People were so quick to be upset with the guy in the relationship for causing adversity, but why not be upset with the female for allowing it? People only do what they're allowed. The dean didn't allow her to sell drugs on his campus, so she was thrown out. If he would've allowed it she'd still be on campus selling drugs. Tae personally didn't feel bad for Syren.

"No problem. I'll see you when we get back."

***

Syren was so disheveled. An hour had passed since the boys and Tae left, yet she was still fully dressed like she was going somewhere. Her heart ached like an elderly widow who just lost her husband of thirty years. Maine was really outdoing himself. To disappoint her was one thing, but to do so to their son was another. Jaelyn was so excited to go that he didn't care if he went alone.

Syren needed someone to talk to. Not a friend, not Kreesha, but someone of relevance: her mother. She pressed the phone against her ear in hopes that she would answer. Her mother laid down early and awoke early. 8:17 was actually past her bedtime.

"Hey Momma," Syren said, trying to sound cheerful.

"Hey baby, what's going on?"

"I'm okay. What you doing up?"

"I was thirsty. I got up and grabbed me something to drink. How's my son and grandson?" she continued.

"Momma, I'm tired."

"Tired of what, baby?"

"Jermaine been staying out all night, lying, and not answering——"

"Stop, Syren. Baby, you're not tired, 'cause when you really tired, you don't need to convince me because you don't even speak on it. Tell my son and grandson I said hello and I love them. I love you too, sweetie. I'm about to go to bed. Bring Jaelyn to see me when you can."

Click!

Syren peered down at the screen in shock. *How could my mother disconnect the call when I'm in such a desperate situation?* Syren thought.

Pissed, she rose to her feet and went into the kitchen. Eating always made her feel better.

Knock! Knock! Knock!

She jumped at the sound of the noise, nearly dropping the glass in her hand. The knock wasn't normal. It was urgent, which instantly made Syren nervous.

Maybe it's the police.

She peered out of the peephole at a frightened and shaky Angie. She swiftly unlocked the locks and opened the door.

"Angie? What——"

"Look, I can't-I can't do this anymore," she stammered before bursting out in tears. She wrapped her arms around Syren, burying her face into her chest.

Syren hugged her back, stroking her hair gently. "Just come on in, Angie," she said, guiding her into her home. "Talk to me. What's going on?"

"He beats me for everything. Every single thing, Syren," she spoke in between sniffles. The tears flowed down her smooth skin rapidly.

Instantly sympathizing, Syren felt the warm, salty liquid descend down her cheeks into the corners of her mouth. Angie didn't deserve the pain she was enduring. She was a beautiful woman, both inside and out. "Do you want to go get some of your things?"

"Uh-uh!" Angie shook her head swiftly. "He's in a rage and I fear he might take me out this time," she continued. She stood there shaking like a leaf.

"Damn, Angie, that's serious shit, girl."

Angie nodded her head, using the back of her hand to wipe the snot from her nose.

As an outsider looking in, you never would've thought it. Brandon possessed a smooth and laid back demeanor. Although he rarely came to any of the social gatherings Maine and Syren orchestrated, the one time he did he was very social and calm. He cracked jokes and laughed most of the time. He didn't appear to be clingy and he catered to Angie's every need. But looks could be deceiving.

"Look, Angie, you can stay here as long as you need to. I'm so sorry you're going through this mess, friend, but I'm here and I love you."

"Thanks, Syren."

"Come on," Syren said, pulling her into a hug before leading her into an empty bedroom. Although there was only a twin size bed and a 19" TV in the spacious room, it was better than returning home and facing that demon.

"I'll be back," Syren said, making her way down the hall and up the stairs into her bedroom. She retrieved her money green robe, two sets of satin pajamas, and three new pairs of boy shorts she purchased from Victoria's Secret to give to Angie.

"Hey Angie, I got——" She paused. "Angie?" she called out, peering around the empty room. She strolled down the hallway, noticing the light from underneath the restroom door. She was about to knock when she realized the door wasn't shut all the way. "Hey Angie! Angie! No! Angie, wait!"

Syren's eyes widened in distress and her piercing scream echoed throughout the house. Angie sat on the edge of the tub with blood leaking from her bare thighs and wrist. She continued to use the sharp kitchen knife to slice her skin. Syren rushed her and grabbed the weapon, and without a fight, she let go. Chucking the bloody knife into the sink, she peered down at Angie, mystified. If Syren didn't know the extent of Angie's misery, she did now.

"Really, Angie? Really!"

"You don't understand, Syren. It's dreadful. The physical and verbal abuse have taken a toll on me. The things he says are demented and despicable and I'm afraid of what he might do next. I love him more than I love myself. To escape the pain and gain peace, I'd rather die," she whispered breathlessly.

"You're talking nonsense. Some of those cuts are old, Angie."

"I've cut before. I do it quite often. Just in the inside of my thighs to keep people from noticing. But today I'm not cutting to solace the pain. I want it to be over," she confessed, peering down at the tile floor.

Syren rummaged through the counter, grabbing the peroxide and gauze pads. The cuts weren't as deep as they appeared. There was just a lot of blood. She used a baby wipe to clean around the cut after pouring the peroxide on top of it. She then used the clear medical tape to bandage it, wrapping it tight enough so that the water wouldn't seep in.

"Look, Angie, I'm not going to monitor you like you're in some sort of psych ward, but I'm going to say this. It's other people in this world that love you as much as he do. You can't give up on yourself or them, 'cause, we will never give up on you. If he loves you so much, he wouldn't cause so much pain in your life. Love isn't supposed to hurt."

Syren grabbed the bloody towel and walked out of the restroom. She headed back down the hall towards the kitchen when a noise summoned her attention, compelling her to slow her stride. She peered out the living room window, spotting Maine walking up the driveway. He used his hand to swipe away whatever appeared to be on his shirt. Syren ran and sat in the love seat. Seconds later, the locks turned and the door opened. Maine stepped inside. She couldn't wait to see his expression when he flicked the light switch and saw her wide awake, awaiting his return. To her surprise, he locked the locks and headed down the long hallway.

I can't believe this nigga.

She hopped up and followed behind him. She was livid, and the pace of her walk made it clear.

"Maine, so you just——" She gasped, shielding her mouth. The hair on the back of her neck stood at attention while she stared at Maine, wide-eyed and terrified.

"I got robbed, Syren, for everything." His lips were swollen and leaking blood, and his left eye was nearly closed. His eyelid was so puffy it almost covered his entire eye, which drooped all the way down to his eyebone.

"But wh-what happened?" she stammered, never looking away. She softly placed both hands on his face, searching his eyes.

"I was getting gas——"

"Sit down," she said, helping him onto the edge of the bed.

"I was getting gas on my way home when two dudes approached me, then put a gun to my head. When they realized all I had was three hundred and a ticket to the game, they started beating me with the butt of the gun. Someone walked up and they took off."

"Why didn't you call me?"

"I didn't want to worry you. Honestly, I thought you went to the game. It didn't seem that bad until I saw my eye. I rushed home after leaving the police station to see if I still had enough time to make it to the game."

"Fuck that game! Look at your face! And besides, they left two hours ago. I thought you were out messing around and left me and Jaelyn high and dry."

"I would never let you guys down," Maine promised her before leaning down and kissing her lips.

"Come on, let's get you cleaned up."

While attending to Maine's wounds, Syren informed him of Angie's arrival and briefly spoke on her situation.

Chapter 8
How deep is your love?

"Damn!" Dekari yelled as soon as he walked through the door.

"Man, De, I did the same shit when he woke me up this morning," Tae voiced.

"What happened? Damn, a nigga come in on you fucking his bitch? 'Cause I know that's where you were."

"I was." Maine grinned mischievously.

"So?"

"Well, once I realized I lost track of time, I knew this would be the straw that broke the camel's back and Syren would leave me. So I got Uh'Nija to hit me in my shit a few times with a blow dryer."

"Uh'Nija?" both Tae and Dekari voiced in unison with a look of disgust.

"You low-key love that ho," Dekari commented. "You missed time with yo' family for Uh'Nija? How the hell you lose track of time, nigga? Look at yo' face. All that, when you could've just shown up," Dekari continued, certainly displeased.

"Check this: she told me she had a surprise for me." He paused waiting for Dekari to speak.

"What?" he asked nonchalantly, rolling his eyes.

"This stallion...oooh-weee, she was bad! She walked through the door, removed her trench coat, and nothing underneath but skin——"

"Nigga, it wasn't Meagan."

"No, it wasn't Meagan - not by herself. But the other girl was a stallion...a stallion! Anyways, they freaked me up and down like they were auditioning for a porno."

"So that was worth you looking like George Foreman after Ali kicked his ass?" Dekari asked, reclining in the leather chair.

Maine slowly nodded his head in approval. "Look, I already decided. I'm going to drive to the H. and take Jaelyn to see Harden and Lillard go at it next week."

"He'll be at practice," Dekari stated.

"Nah, weekdays only, fam."

"I asked you if I could put him AAU, which automatically suppresses him from playing for his school, 'cause practice is the same time and they have gatherings on weekends."

"Oh, okay, I forgot about that. I'll figure something out then."

The door to the office opened and instantly Maine's smile faded.

"Hey y'all, I got the money."

"Dra'Neisha?" Tae asked curiously.

"It's Draco," she corrected, squinting.

"Bre'untae?" Draco asked.

"It's Tae. What's good, baby?"

"What's up!" she yelled as they embraced each other tightly.

"Where you been? I was looking for you on the Gram and the Book," Tae said.

"Oh, I don't do social media, fam. It'll fuck you legally and personally. It is good for business though."

"You right. You look good."

"'Preciate it. You do too"

"Ahem." Maine cleared his throat

"Excuse me, Tae. Hey, I was coming by to tell you I have the rent plus an extra $200."

"That's good, but you late, man. I told you yesterday."

"I called, Bossman, but you didn't pick up."

"That's a lie. "

"I'm telling you——"

"You had a deadline that you didn't meet. I'm going to need you to gather your belongings and vacate the apartment ASAP. You refuse to comply, I'll help you."

As soon as the words fell from Maine's mouth, Draco's slightly ajar mouth closed. She sighed deeply, dropping her head in defeat before walking out.

"Draco!" Tae called out, following behind her.

"You could've let ol' girl make it," Dekari suggested.

"Fuck that. It's clear she don't have a set income and she'll just come in here begging for an extension next month. I do enough of that with Kreesha's fat ass."

"You right. Fuck it." Dekari shrugged.

"Damn, you ruthless," Tae said, walking in.

"It's business, sis."

"But bruh, that bitch Karma is real. She'll get you everytime. That ho will ride on your passenger side, eat at the table with you, sleep with you, shower, shit, and shave with you. She don't miss a beat."

"If I don't do right by the bitch that has my heart, I surely don't give a fuck about the next bitch," Maine said.

***

"Wait, wait," Kreesha whispered, breathing heavily as Chris backed her into the stall inside of the restaurant's women's restroom.

She had been fixing her makeup in the large mirror when Chris barged inside and shoved his long, thick tongue down her throat. His tongue tasted like both alcohol and smoke, but his lips were soft as cotton candy and juicy as a warm peach.

He used one hand to open the door to the stall while his other hand caressed her all over.

"Put one leg on the toilet," he demanded.

"Chris," she protested.

"Come on and give me my pussy."

She peered into his eyes, admiring his muscles that bulged underneath his shirt. She loved the burning desire he had for her and only her. She propped one leg on the toilet while he unbuckled his Guess jeans, whipping his massive penis out. The sight of it made her mouth water. Even the veins that protruded were sexy. She was starting to drool when she felt the tip of his man at her opening. Before she could speak, he slid into her wetness and slowly stroked her kitty.

"Ooohh, Chris," she whined. The pain and pleasurable feeling was electrifying, forcing her to buck her hips.

"Yeah, just like that." Chris strained while quickening his pace.

The door to the restroom burst open and she made eye contact with an elderly woman and a young girl.

"I don't give a damn who's watching, you better not stop" Chris demanded through clenched teeth, biting her savagely on the shoulder.

"Aaaaghh!" she shrieked. "Okay, okay, Chris," she begged as he continued to pump vigorously.

He pulled back, releasing the grip he had on her shoulder with his teeth. Kreesha reached up to caress the bite mark, but was taken back when she felt the warm liquid. She looked with panic at the blood that covered her fingers.

"Fuck me back, or I'm going to do it again," he threatened.

Kreesha honestly wanted Chris to do it again, but she wasn't going to tell him that.

"Just like that! I'm cumming," he voiced.

She swirled the tip and jerked her hips as if they were both listening to the same tune. They rode the beat effortlessly. She knew Chris was on the verge of cumming when his body began to stiffen and his veins protruded from his neck. On cue, she placed her hand over his mouth, muffling the roar. He pulled out and busted all over her thigh before collapsing onto her chest, breathing heavily, like a runaway slave.

She mumbled to Chris, "Bae, we can't do this here."

"You right," he whispered, adjusting his clothes.

She used the large, brown paper towels to wipe the semen off her leg before making her exit.

She and Chris went back to their table, making unintentional eye contact with the lady and her daughter who had come into the restroom. Kreesha quickly lowered her head and kept walking. She noticed a few more lingering eyes, but thought nothing of it.

"Am I tripping, or——" Chris started.

"No, you not. Let's eat someplace else," she chimed in.

Ashamed, Kreesha and Chris left the Applebees and headed across the street to Olive Garden.

***

"Ooooh, I can't wait to squeeze my fat ass into that dress," Kreesha voiced loudly, killing the engine.

"It is cute. Chris going to make you come out of that," Uh'Nija responded, unlocking the door to her apartment.

The sound of Chris's name made her heart skip a beat. She was feeling him, no doubt. "Are you going to do my makeup, or should I ask Syren?"

"Bitch, you know it takes me an hour to do mine, but if you don't mind the wait, I got you." She paused. "So which one of your niggas gave you chlamydia?"

"You don't know him. He's from the west."

"Okay." She peered at Uh'Nija suspiciously, trying to get her to admit to the affair with Maine. She decided to drop the topic until later.

The Louis Vuitton headband hugged Kreesha's forehead a bit tightly, but she refused to remove it. After borrowing the headband from Syren, she decided to switch her attire up. Instead of the short Fashion Nova dress, she decided to wear a knock-off Louis Vuitton belt, collared shirt, and skinny jeans. The brown slightly-pointed boots had been purchased for just twenty dollars at the beauty supply store. They resembled the ones at Aldo's, so she hoped no one would notice. The only thing authentic on Kreesha was the headband. She was a knock-off queen. Being a single parent to teenaged kids, there was no way she could afford the real stuff.

"Bitch, it look like you about to bust out of that shirt," Uh'Nija commented.

"It is a li'l tight. But damn, I don't want to wear anything loose. You commenting and shit. Help a bitch out and let me wear your waist trainer. "

"Sure, the one that's altered to fit me!" she shot back sarcastically.

"Ok, you got plastic wrap and tape?"

"Yeah, it's some in the pantry. Bitch, you doing too much."

"Bitch your stomach on flat, flat. I'm trying to get like you, what you mad about?" Kreesha said while retrieving the wrap.

"It's just ratchet."

"It's cool, we all got some ratchet in us. Come on," Kreesha said holding the plastic wrap and tape up.

Uh'Nija raised up from her stool that was connected to her vanity, playfully snatching the items out of her hand.

The nerve of this bitch to call me ratchet and she's fucking her friend's husband, Kreesha thought.

"Hold your shirt up at the back," she instructed, carefully wrapping Kreesha's fat. After wrapping the plastic around her midsection four times, she placed a piece of tape to secure the wrap. "You on now," Uh'Nija said, gawking at the huge difference.

"Thank you. And your makeup is flawless," Kreesha complimented her while admiring the precise brows and the exquisite colored eyeshadow. She wore just enough highlight to complete her look.

"Thanks, girl," she said, taking another glance in the mirror. "Okay, come on."

Kreesha pulled her thirty-two-inch loose wave bundles back into a low ponytail, allowing Uh'Nija greater access to do her thing. Thirty minutes later, she was glancing back at her own reflection and boy, it was something to stare at.

The cotton candy pink eyeshadow was stunning, but subtle. The neutral brown at the end of her eyes enhanced the makeup, making her eyes appear bigger. The matte pink lipstick matched the eye shadow, and since she used the Bare Minerals foundation, you could hardly tell she had any on.

"You beautiful, baby," Uh'Nija said, walking away, only to return a minute later with her clutch and car keys. "You ready?" she asked.

"Yes," Kreesha responded, never looking away from the mirror.

"Well, get out the damn mirror. Let's go."

Kreesha slowly rose to her feet while continuously stealing glances. "Okay, okay," she said, walking to the couch to retrieve her knock-off Louis Vuitton bag.

"Damn, girl," she blurted after doing a double take. Uh'Nija's Chanel leggings and crop top hugged her body to perfection. The outfit truly complemented her slim figure, magnifying her bubble butt. Her blonde pixie cut gave her an exotic look, but the smoke grey thigh-high boots is what really set off the entire 'fit.

"Yeah, I'm trying to shut some shit down," Uh'Nija stated.

"Oh, you definitely are." *Broke pussy and all,* Kreesha thought.

"Momma, can Marcus come in?" De'erick asked, walking up Uh'Nija's breezeway.

"De'erick, you and Meagan better not have anybody in my house while I'm gone," she responded

De'erick smacked his lips before walking away. "Come on, Momma, please?" He stopped, then turned around.

"I said no! Y'all won't get to turn my shit into no hookah lounge," she said, opening Uh'Nija's passenger door and hopping in.

***

"Over here, y'all!" Syren waved from the VIP section.

Club Elite was for the grown and sexy, eighteen and up. Kreesha's type of setting. The twenty-five and under crowd was a bit too hype for her. She grabbed Uh'Nija's hand and they made their way toward everyone else. It was crowded, but not to the point where they had to turn sideways and say "Excuse me" a thousand times to get from one side to the next.

"Hey y'all," Kreesha announced, hugging Syren. They embraced each other tightly, yet you could tell Syren had been drinking.

"Hey De, Maine, Snoop, Jerry...and you are?" Kreesha asked, peering at Tae, whom she thought was absolutely attractive. Her skin resembled the top of a Reeses peanut butter cup. Smooth without blemishes of any sort. The kush made her eyes appear chinky.

"I'm Tae," she said. "Maine's sister," she continued, Kreesha looked dumbfounded.

"That's Bre'untae, Kreesha," Syren intervened.

"Bre'untae? Damn, it's been a minute. You look totally different."

Tae responded with a slight chuckle, revealing her deep dimples.

Uh'Nija sat beside Dekari, pouring herself a glass of the expensive liquor that sat on the table. Mingling with him and Tae, she eyed Maine discreetly.

"Syren!" Kreesha called out.

"What's up, cuz?" she slurred.

"You alright?"

"I'm great, how about yourself? You look amazing!"

"Thanks. Uh'Nija did my makeup. Hey, I wanted to let you in on something," Kreesha spoke softly, peering around. "You do know why that bitch went to the clinic the other day right?" Kreesha continued.

"She's pregnant."

"Hell no! She has chlamydia," she revealed. Kreesha stared at Syren, awaiting her response, hoping her green ass would catch on.

"For real? Damn, chlamydia just running rampant, huh? You didn't tell anyone about me having it, did you?"

"Hell no!" Kreesha responded, tossing the shot back. Syren was so damn naive sometimes. She wondered how she made it through thirty long years.

Meagan the Stallion's "Savage" lyrics blarred through the speakers.

"Come on, Syren! Come on Nija!" Kreesha yelled, strutting to the dance floor.

Syren and Nija followed close behind. Full of liquor, Kreesha rode that beat, throwing the long Peruvian over her shoulders. She threw her ass in a square because she surely couldn't throw it in a circle. Syren was a bit too tipsy, but she was showing her ass. Literally. She twerked to the beat fluently, better than a lot of the younger females. As an adolescent, dancing was just something Syren was always talented at, and she never lost her touch. The short tight Dior dress ascended with every pop. In fear for her, Kreesha glanced back to Maine to see if he was on his way to drag her off the floor, which he done a few times before because he was upset at all the attention she was receiving. She couldn't tell exactly what he was looking at, due to the Gucci shades he wore, but she knew he could possibly have been looking at his wife.

She peered behind her at Uh'Nija, who wasn't just twerking. She was trying to hypnotize someone with the way she moved seductively. The moves she was executing were ones similar to a stripper. She bent down and grabbed both ankles making her ass clap like a proud parent on graduation day. She looked back and Kreesha assumed she was eyeing Maine until she signaled Tae to come over. However, Tae shook her head no and continued to nurse the drink in her hand. Out of Kreesha's peripheral vision, she spotted Dekari pointing and whispering something into Maine's ear. On cue, he hopped off the sectional and marched onto the dance floor.

Kreesha peeped Uh'Nija and Tae talking by the bar. She flashed a look of disgust, turning her attention back to the enraged Maine, who had Syren snatched up by the arm.

"Chill, Maine, what's going on?" Kreesha asked, full of concern.

"Shut up, Kreesha. You see that naked ass; you know what's going on. She struttin' around here like a ho!" he hollered.

"That's what you like, nigga," Syren murmured. Syren looked like she didn't have a care in this world, rolling her eyes at Maine, snapping her fingers to the beat.

"Kreesha, take her home before I kill her motherfuckin' ass."

"No, I'm staying." She attempted to jerk away. "I'm having fun," she slurred.

"Uh-uh, Maine, I'm not ready to go. I just got here," she whined. The night had just begun and Kreesha wasn't ready to leave.

"I'll take her, fam. I'm ready to go anyways," Tae chimed in.

"Bet. Take the car. I'll get Dekari to drop me off."

Ah'Million

Chapter 9
By any means, chase that bag

"Come on, man," Tae said, passing a tipsy Syren, proceeding to the exit.

"Hold on, Tae!" Syren yelled, sauntering towards her.

Tae deeply exhaled while waiting patiently. Syren sloppily draped her arm over Tae's shoulder, immediately forcing the left side of her top lip to curl upward. She didn't want Syren's drunk ass on her.

Tae felt the cool breeze brush her face as soon as she stepped out onto the pavement. Syren became dependent with each step, but Tae remained tight-lipped, not wanting to muster up any conversation whatsoever.

"Damn," a brown-skinned chick uttered to her friend impulsively once Tae appeared in her view. The two chicks stared her down and Tae returned the bold gesture. The friend wasn't all that hot in Tae's eyes, but the chick who made the comment was gorgeous. Her face was beat to perfection. Tae just hoped she looked the same once she removed the MAC.

"That's you?" the brown-skinned chick asked, insinuating Syren was her chick.

"Hell nah, this my——"

Vomit flew out of Syren's mouth like the possessed chick on the *Exorcist*. Luckily, it missed Tae's Fendi 'fit. However, it did land all over her Louis Vuitton sneakers.

"Come on, man, damn!" she voiced outraged.

The chick and her friend peered at Tae in disgust. They mumbled to each other before walking off. Tae's nose flared and she pressed her lips together, annoyed by the despicable sight. She stood there with her hands on her hips, looking around for nothing in particular.

"I'm sorry," Syren said, peering up at Tae, bent over. She stood up straight, wiping the vomit from her mouth, which she did a poor job of. She didn't even bother to remove the streak of vomit on her cheekbone.

Tae grabbed her by the arm and treaded over the vomit, practically dragging Syren. Once they made it to Maine's Camaro, Tae untied her sneakers, removed them, then tossed them across the street.

"Bruh, get in. You not *that* drunk that you need assistance to open the door!" Tae snapped, climbing inside the vehicle.

"I could've cleaned those for you," Syren spoke breathlessly, flopping down onto her seat.

"You couldn't have did shit but what you doing. I'll buy some more and you giving me half. Them shits cost me $1200," Tae argued, pressing the start button.

The sound of car doors caught her attention. She looked to the left at an expensively dressed couple headed for the club. The black on black Bentley truck looked like something out of the movies. They were engrossed in a deep conversation, seemingly an argument. Tae waited for the alarm to sound, but it never did.

"Hold on——" Tae decided against saying anything to Syren since she was extremely drunk.

Once the couple was inside, she hopped out of the car and walked both calmly and smoothly to the driver's side of the truck. Her heart raced as she pulled on the handle, hoping the alarm wouldn't sound, and it didn't. She climbed inside, swiftly peering back, making it difficult to see without light. She used the lit screen on her phone, but it wasn't much help. She felt under the driver's seat. It was empty, and so was the glove compartment, surprisingly. She was starting to believe the car was a rental. Lastly, she reached underneath the seat in the backseat.

Bingo! She snatched the purse from underneath the seat, but not before Syren peaked her head inside.

"What the fuck you doing?" Syren asked.

"Get out the way and get your drunk ass back in the car!" Tae yelled.

"I was just trying to help your scary ass," she huffed before slamming the door shut.

Tae climbed out, eased the door closed, and strolled back to Maine's car. Once inside, she flicked the lights and searched the purse quickly but thoroughly. The makeup products held no significance, but inside the zipper held eighteen hundred in cash. She stuffed the money in her pocket and continued to rummage. The wallet inside was smaller than most. No cash; just a few cards. A driver's license, Victoria's Secret gift card, Cash App card, bank and gas card, along with the Social Security card. Everything else was irrelevant. She tossed the purse in the backseat and swerved out of the lot.

"So that's how you make your bread?" Syren spoke in a low tone.

"Don't worry about it. Why you get out the car?"

"I was trying to tell you the security was driving around. I see you got your shoe money."

"I don't need you paying attention to my pockets 'cause you still giving me my six, bruh."

"All right," she dragged.

Tae sped to the house.

"Come on. You think you can walk on your own?"

"I got it. You don't want to help a bitch anyways."

"I'm glad you figured that out!" Tae shot back.

As soon as her toes stepped into wet grass, she grew upset all over again. She eyed Syren from a distance until she made it to the porch.

Tae's phone rang just as she got to the front door.

111

"Hello," she answered.

"Hey baby," Iesha whispered.

"How you holding up, mama? I was just thinking about you," Tae said, stopping abruptly, cherishing the sound of her voice. She believed being away from Iesha was another reason she had been so edgy. She truly missed her chick.

Syren undressed while proceeding upstairs. She turned in the opposite direction.

"You not fucking around on me, are you?"

"Come on, Iesha don't start with that. Maine's chick done already fucked my night up."

"How?"

Tae went on explaining everything that had taken place and heard Syren vomiting from a distance. She quickly but soundlessly made her way up the stairs, careful not to wake Angie or Jaelyn. She spotted Syren squatted down, leaning over the toilet. She grimaced while clutching her stomach in pain. Tae noticed the thin streaks of vomit in her hair.

"Bae, call me back, it's vomit everywhere. I love you."

Click!

She pulled Syren's hair back, removing the rubber band that was placed around the stack of money in her pocket. She placed her hair in a loose ponytail. Syren was beautiful even during an ugly situation. Her skin was defectless and smooth. The lime green bra and panties looked remarkable on her, but there had to be something she was lacking to lose Maine's attention. Then again, Maine was trash. Just like most men. Maine and his friends were one of the reasons Tae decided she wanted to be with a woman.

"Look, I'm going to turn this water on. Just sit in it. I'm not helping you undress. You can fall asleep if all I care. At least you'll be good and sober tomorrow," Tae voiced.

Tae set her phone on the counter and helped Syren to her feet. She guided her to the tub and carefully helped Syren to her feet, then helped her inside. Syren reached for her underwear in an attempt to pull them off.

"Hold on, hold on," Tae objected.

"Girl, calm down, you got what I got."

"I don't give a—— Better yet, I'm out."

"Tae!" she called out. Tae turned around. "Thanks."

"Nah, you good, I was just helping Maine."

Tae eased out the door and down the steps. Remembering the stolen purse, she jogged to the car to retrieve it.

Syren and Maine had a beautiful fireplace in the front room. Tae removed her T-shirt and jeans. Dressed in just a Fruit of the Loom tank top and black briefs, she sat on the cushioned love seat directly in front of the blazing fire. Everything left inside with the exception of the cards she tossed inside, watching it melt slowly. Once she was done with the items, she was about to toss the bag until she realized it was Balenciaga.

"Hmmm."

She climbed the stairs two at a time then peaked inside the restroom, but it was empty. She softly knocked on Syren's bedroom door.

"Your mustache." Tae pointed at the milk above Syren's upper lip.

"Oh. I'm trying to sober up."

Her hair had been washed. The loose waves seemed tighter and her makeup was gone, yet her beauty remained. Although her robe was tied tightly at her waist, you could still see a glimpse of cleavage.

"Hey, you want this?"

"That stolen bag?" Syren mugged her.

"Yeah. It's Balenciaga."

113

"But it's——"

"Don't worry about it. Your stuck up ass always trying to look down on something," Tae said, storming off.

"Psst! Psst!"

Tae stopped and turned around slowly. "Yeah, man."

"I want it," she said.

Tae handed her the bag and descended the steps. Before heading to shower, she peeked in on Jaelyn. He was wide awake playing a video game. The volume was extremely low because all you could hear was the buttons being pressed. She started to join him, but thought against it after remembering the early morning meeting she had scheduled with Draco. She left unnoticed, eased the door closed, and hopped in the shower.

***

Tae sat in the apartment office with both Dekari and Maine the next morning, waiting for Draco to arrive. She didn't want to conduct business in the office, knowing Maine and Draco weren't too fond of each other. Tae had known Draco when she was referred to as Dra'Neisha. Even in her younger days, she liked females. Draco and Tae were both on the school's basketball team. Draco actually made being gay cool when so many people sneered at the idea. People like that made Tae hide the desire she had for women for a long time. So many girls at school were attracted to Draco. Perhaps it was her blue eyes and naturally curly blonde hair. She almost resembled Drake's son Adonis. She was mixed with Australian and black and her skin was the color of buttered popcorn. She had full pink lips and extremely long lashes.

Draco liked the fact that Tae didn't like her like the other females. She soon found out that Tae was attracted to the same

114

thing she was attracted to: women. Draco got into a little trouble before graduation, which threw a wrench in their college plans. She ended up doing a small bid in the county jail, which automatically forfeited her scholarship. Tae could've held her down a little longer, but she didn't. She did write her once or twice and send a few throwback pictures of them on the team, but that was it. However, upon Draco's release, she never tried contacting Tae either.

A guy strolled into the office. Dekari and Tae shared the same look of confusion once he bypassed them. Maine didn't seem bothered. The guy scanned the room through beady eyes as he approached Maine's desk.

"What's up, man? Maine asked, smirking.

"I'm good, I'm good," he replied, fidgeting, steadily peering around while digging inside his pockets. He pulled out a few crisp bills before handing them to Maine.

"'Preciate you. I got you as soon as it clear out," Maine assured him.

Instead of leaving, the man stood there for a moment, hands tucked away in his pockets.

"I said I got you, bruh."

"Yeah, I know, but do you know when exactly?" he asked.

"I got you tomorrow," Maine stated aggressively.

Without a response, the guy turned around and walked out. He seemed upset, as if he wanted to speak, but had decided against it.

*****

"Okay, don't worry about nothing, baby, I got you. My people on it right now," Draco said, reassuring Tae. Draco was a jack of all trades, but lately things had been rocky. Every time she got a step ahead, something knocked her two steps back. *Everyone so selfish and inconsiderate, like that bitch ass nigga Maine,* she thought.

Draco believed she knew why he was upset. She didn't know it then, but had recently found out that Uh'Nija wasn't just a tenant. She and Maine were creeping. However, everyone knew Uh'Nija had it bad for Draco. Not downplaying the feelings she had for Uh'Nija, but to Draco Uh'Nija was just entertainment.

Uh'Nija was too demanding. Since Draco's swag spoke volumes, females automatically assumed her money was long. At times it was, but lately, nothing had been consistent. Every true hustler knows there's high and lows. Every day isn't a good one. Their last conversation, Uh'Nija asked her for a Chanel bag - not the one you find at a bazaar or flea market either. The bag was eighty-five hundred and it wasn't no bigger than the palm of her hand. She hadn't spoken to Uh'Nija since. Females could be so ignorant at times. They want an expensive-ass bag, but what's going inside? Gum?

The women in Draco's life didn't live long lives, but the years they were there, they taught her a few things of relevance that held significance. When she was twelve, her grandma and mother were both taken away from her at the same time in a deadly car crash. Her dad was somewhere in the Philippines, on the run. He was still on the Most Wanted list to this day. Her mother explained to her the reason why her father was running. With all he had going on, Draco would've fled too without looking back. The absence of her two favorite women was a huge part of the reason she began pursuing females. Before she was adopted by her foster parents, she went from one foster home to the next, vulnerable, curious, confused, and lonely. She became even more attracted to women, and being around them all the time only made her desire them more. Before unveiling her sexuality, she had a bad habit of watching and mentally undressing them. She would whine and refused to take baths unless she was given a shower buddy. It wasn't hard for Draco to bag chicks then. They were suckas for her ocean blue eyes. Eventually, she was adopted by her foster parents, a Caucasian family, who still loved her dearly and genuinely.

The vibration from her iPhone caught her attention. She retrieved it from the cup holder and read the new message.

Tangy: she not worth shit but she do have 6k Instagram followers.

Draco: preciate you baby I got you.

"Hey fam, she don't have any credit, but she do have six thousand in her bank account."

Draco and Tangy always talked and texted in code just in case the Feds were watching. Tangy was a snow bunny Draco used to mess with. According to Draco, Tangy was the truth. She know exactly how to talk to, treat, and sex her. Draco never had to tell her what to do because it was already done, and if anything was displeasing, she would inquire until it was perfected. There was just one flaw - one of the same flaws, most women possess. Availability. At the time, Draco had no plans of settling down. In Tangy's eyes, they were a couple. Draco had a need, and she met it. Joyfully, she didn't trip, ask questions, or stay mad, which gave Draco permission to do her thing, knowing Tangy would stay down through whatever - which Draco honestly found distasteful.

Draco did begin to give her a tad bit more love, affection, attention, and even gifts on the strength of Tangy being so fabulous to her. By that time Tangy was head over heels, wanting to take things to the next level. Marriage - something

Draco couldn't commit to. She knew she couldn't marry Tangy if she had never given her all to Tangy. Tangy was hurt by the decision, but Draco had to keep it one hundred. Her name wouldn't be Draco if she would have done the opposite. Although she did truly care about Tangy, since she couldn't give her what she desired, Draco pulled back, forcing her to find the strength to press forward on her own. She hated Draco for a long time - until months after the fact. Draco asked her out to eat and broke everything down to her. They had been cool ever since. Sometimes boundaries were overstepped because Tangy was undeniably fine, but for the most part, they had an understanding.

"Okay, how we gon' get it? Neither one of us looks like this bitch," Tae said.

"Let me worry about that, fam. This time tomorrow, I'm going to have the loot," promised Draco.

Tae rubbed her hands together while grinning mischievously.

"I like the sound of that. Where you headed?"

"Man, I don't know. Maine wrong than a bitch. He could've let me keep my apartment, man." Draco was so livid and upset. She wanted to cry. Although her money had been funny, she busted her ass to get that rent money. She damn near thought she would have to sell some ass to get it.

"Man, my brother just real stern when it comes to his money. I apologize for his lack of consideration, but tomorrow you'll have some money for a deposit and first month rent 'cause I'm busting it down the middle."

"That's some real shit, and anytime you get your hands on something like that, I got you."

"Okay. Pull over there to my sister's shop. Let me check something out. She want me to come cut hair 'cause she don't have a barber. "

"Bet."

Tae and Draco strolled inside the beauty shop. More than a few women, along with a couple kids. occupied the inside. The place had a refreshing, yet feminine setting. The walls were hot pink and turquoise. The lights were extremely bright and it smelled like Bath and Body Works. Mistakingly, Draco made eye contact with Uh'Nija's ass, instantly altering her mood. All eyes were on them, but the only person Draco was focused on was the brown-skinned chick that stood before her.

"Hey Tae, hey Tae's friend," Syren greeted. "I'm Syren, and this is Syren's Salon," she continued.

Draco undressed her with her eyes, daring Syren to address the matter.

"What's up, Syren? I just came to peep the scene and check out the set up."

"Do you mind if I show her around, Syren?" Uh'Nija asked.

Draco rolled her eyes at the slut. Little did Uh'Nija know, Draco wanted a little alone time with the beauty who owned the place.

"Go ahead," she agreed, scowling slightly at Uh'Nija's friendly gesture.

As soon as Draco opened her mouth to speak, Syren gave her a tight-lipped smile before walking off.

The ones that never been with a woman always give me a hard time in the beginning, but with time and persistence, they soften like ass shots.

Ah'Million

Chapter 10
Can't even trust ya own family at times

"So, bitch, you gon' fuck the sister too?" Kreesha asked Uh'Nija.

"What you mean too?"

"Exactly what I said. Girl, everyone but Syren know you and Maine are fucking."

"That's not true," Uh'Nija protested weakly.

"Okay, whatever."

"You think I'm wrong?"

"Dead ass wrong," Kreesha stated. "You benefiting, bitch?" she continued.

"Of course. He started, fattening my pockets" Uh'Nija boasted, downing the drink. She had invited Kreesha over for breakfast after the crazy night they had.

"Let a bitch hold something," Kreesha pressed.

"How much you need?"

"Just two hundred and fifty dollars," Kreesha requested.

"You said 'just' like you meant two dollars and fifty cent, instead of two hundred and fifty."

"Come on, you got it."

"I guess. But if you knew, why haven't you told Syren?" Uh'Nija inquired.

"You my bitch. I mean, that is my cousin, but friends can be closer than relatives. It's biblically proven."

"Well, we were into it a few days ago, but now we're fine."

"Yeah, I saw the stunt he pulled," she said, peering over to her glass.

"What stunt?" Uh'Nija asked, dumbfounded.

"Making Syren leave so y'all could chill. I did stay, remember?"

Uh'Nija rolled her eyes while trying to hide the huge grin on her face. She really enjoyed her lifestyle - the zero guarantee and no expectations or responsibilities.

"Kreesha, you must understand, I play second because there are no strings nor commitment. When he's not in my bed, another nigga is - or maybe I'm enjoying me time. Sometimes I tend to get in my feelings, but I don't drown in them. Syren is the one restless, hurt, betrayed, feeling abandoned and misused. Not me. Love is painful. I play my role, reap the benefits, and do me."

"That's sensible. I'll catch up with you later. I got a date with bae."

***

Kreesha was sitting at the bar nursing drink number three when Chris rushed in.

"Baby, I'm sorry I'm late," he apologized, planting kisses on her cheek.

She didn't know if it was the glass of Hennessy, but as soon as he touched her, she melted like ice cream in the month of August.

"It's fine. Join me." Chris sat on the stool next to her as they conversed freely.

They talked more than usual. He was such an attentive listener and always knew the perfect answer.

"You look so beautiful tonight, sweetie," he commented, staring into her eyes.

"Thanks, bae." She blushed.

After all this time Chris and Kreesha had been together. he still had a special effect on her. With both hands he leaned in, gripping her thighs.

"Come on, baby," he begged.

"No, Chris, not here. Let's not do this here," Kreesha protested.

Chris peered at her through narrow slits, searching her eyes for any humor. Kreesha didn't laugh, crack a smile, or anything of that sort. She was tired of sexing him in public and random places and risking being seen and humiliated. If planned, she would never agree to something so degrading, but it always happened in the heat of the moment. He always had a way of talking her out of her panties - if she had any on. She looked at him, refusing to break her stare, but something caught her eye, compelling her to scowl at him. The ring tan on his marriage finger stood out like a sore thumb. She eyed him, then his finger. Chris followed her eyes, realizing what she was looking at. He removed both hands and slowly eased up.

"What's that?" she asked, already knowing the answer.

"What? It's not what you think it is, if that's what you're insinuating."

"Okay, if it's not, let me see it."

"Kreesha——"

"Chris, I want to see it," she demanded cutting him short.

He held up his hand while shifting uncomfortably in his seat.

"You're married aren't you?"

"I was, but——"

"Don't lie to me, Chris. It looked like you just took that off before you walked in."

"No, it's really not like that. We've been separated for months, but I still wear my ring. Sometimes," he claimed. His shoulders sagged in defeat as his eyes shifted back and forth, trying to see if Kreesha was gaining compassion for his saddened spirit.

"You don't give a damn how I feel. Yo' ass just sorry 'cause you got caught. Kiss my ass, Chris," she stated before walking away.

The tears blurred her vision as she leaned up on the steering wheel, trying to focus on the road ahead as she drove away. She thought Chris was the chosen one. He never even showed signs of being a married man. Never did she see this one coming. If a bitch would've tried telling her so, she would've whooped her for lying. Kreesha was mortified.

I knew he wasn't attracted to all of this, she thought, looking into the rearview mirror at herself.

Kreesha arrived to an empty house. She peered down at the time on the screen of her iPhone. 10:26

De'erick and Meagan had phoned her while she was at the restaurant, seeking permission to attend tonight's football game. Supposedly, it was going to be lit. The two schools were rivals - Samuell and Skyline. Permitted or not, she knew the game had ended by now.

In the middle of texting De'erick, a call came through from Uh'Nija.

"Hello?" Kreesha answered.

"Hey bitch. You're early. I just passed your place and noticed your light on."

"Girl, it's a long story."

"Make it short."

"He's married." She sighed before bursting out in tears.

"Awww, baby, I'm sorry. I'm on my way over there. Don't cry, friend. He didn't deserve your sexy ass no way."

"I hate him, I swear I hate him. He could've at least kept it real with me."

"Open the door."

Kreesha opened the door for Uh'Nija, then flopped down onto the couch.

"Uh-uh, what you doing?" Uh'Nija asked from the doorway.

"What you mean?" Kreesha asked, confused.

"Do you know where he lives?"

Ashamedly, Kreesha shook her head no. In the nine months they were together, she hadn't been to his place not even once, which explained the random sex.

"It's nothing to be ashamed about. It's dudes I done fucked with and I can't even tell you their names. Go grab some flour and sugar."

"Huh?"

"Text him and tell him to meet you at the Walmart on 30, and grab some Clorox too."

"What are we about to do? Open a bakery?"

"You'll see. Get the stuff and let's go."

Kreesha grabbed the items and followed Uh'Nija out of the apartment. She marched across the lot, seeming more upset than Kreesha. Kreesha whipped out her phone and shot Chris the text. In a matter of seconds, he replied.

Chris: Ok baby I can't wait 2 c you

"Is that him?" Uh'Nija asked.

"Yeah."

"He thinks his dirty dick ass off the hook. I got something for his lying ass."

"I was looking for y'all motherfuckas. Get in that damn house! Y'all out here posted up like y'all grown!" Kreesha yelled as soon as she spotted Meagan and De'Erick sitting on the hood of the car.

Their heads jerked at the sound of her voice. She heard them mumble something, but there wasn't any hesitation in their strides, so she didn't press the issue.

"So what's the plan?" she asked Uh'Nija again while she raced to Wal-Mart.

"You'll see."

"Is he in a Cadillac Escalade?" Uh'Nija asked, swerving swiftly into the Wal-Mart lot. "Tell me if you see him," she continued, cruising around the almost empty lot.

"He's over there," Kreesha pointed, growing upset at the sight of him.

"Okay, call and tell him something came up and you can't meet him.

"But——"

"Listen to me!" she snapped, hitting the steering wheel.

"Chris, I have to pick up my kids from this game, so I can't meet you right now. I'll just have to wait until tomorrow."

"What are you—— It's fine, bae, no problem." The disappointment in his voice was evident.

"Okay, bye."

Clearly upset, Chris sped out of the lot. Uh'Nija trailed closely but discreetly behind him. Kreesha knew Chris was upset by the way he was driving. He swerved in and out of traffic before veering into a residential area - an area unfamiliar to her. The houses were made of brick and the grass was trimmed and cut to perfection.

Marsh? she thought.

Uh'Nija followed behind Chris on Marsh Street. After seeing him veer inside a driveway, she glanced in his direction, bypassing him and coming to a halt at the stop sign. Seeing Chris made Kreesha's blood boil and heart flutter all at once.

"That was Chris," Kreesha mentioned.

"I know that. Me driving past will kill any suspicion he did have," she explained, turning on the next street, making a circle until she was on Marsh Street again. She parked two to three houses down from Chris's place.

"I'll give him five minutes to unwind," Uh'Nija insisted, picking up the perfectly rolled blunt from the ashtray. She put fire to it and inhaled deeply. "Stimulate ya mind, put a little of this kush in ya tank."

Kreesha and Uh'Nija passed the blunt back and forth. Uh'Nija reached underneath the seat, retrieving a blue funnel.

"Put everything in here," she said, referring to the floral duffle bag."

Kreesha quickly stuffed the flour, sugar, and Clorox inside the duffel bag, including the funnel.

"Okay, bitch, watch out for me. You see a light flick on or you think someone watching me, flash the lights."

Uh'Nija hopped out and jogged down the street. She looked around before placing the bag down and removing the products. She twisted the cap off the Clorox before pouring it all over the jet black Cadillac Escalade. Sweat beads covered her forehead and Kreesha began to panic. The last thing she wanted to see was the inside of a prison cell again.

The gas tank must've been locked because Uh'Nija pulled out some sort of screwdriver from her bag. She tussled with the tank for a minute, or so, before the top came flying off. Sticking the funnel inside the tank, she poured the sugar and flour down the tube all at once. Kreesha was so high-strung she was about to shit on herself

"That'll show his ass," Uh'Nija boasted, hopping inside.

***

"This is nice, bae."

"It's all for you, love," Jermaine quoted, lying on top of the sand with his arms folded underneath his head.

Syren didn't ask the occasion or the reason; she just enjoyed every moment. After eating a nice dinner of Fresh Gulf seafood and listening to Cajun music at one of the local restaurants, they settled on the shores of Sabine Lake. The scenic waterside was amazing and the sand between her toes felt even better. She was dressed in a Missoni one-piece swimsuit and beige Ralph Lauren poncho. Michael Kors wedge heels decorated her feet and the Gucci bucket hat completed her look.

She lay on her side, gazing into Maine's eyes. This was the Maine she knew, met, and loved. The attentive, caring and passionate Maine. His phone rang more than usual. She was about to begin her interrogation when he powered it off.

"I know things been a little off since I broke my promise, but I'm going to make it right," he swore again.

"Let's just enjoy tonight. Don't worry about the past."

He glanced at Syren, gave her a slow nod of approval, and they did exactly what she requested.

***

"Jaelyn, you know tomorrow is a school day. I want you in your bed in thirty minutes."

"But Mom——"

"You heard me, Jaelyn."

He smacked his lips and continued to play his game.

"Don't talk back to your momma. That shit ain't playa," Tae chimed in after pausing the game.

"But I want to stay up and play with you," Jaelyn argued.

"I'm done with school. Finish school and you can do whatever you want. If you don't finish school, you'll be dumb. You ain't gonna get no ho's if you dumb," Tae spoke in a low tone.

"Tae, quit telling my baby that," Syren chimed in. Tae had tried to whisper the last part, but Syren still managed to hear her.

Jaelyn didn't wait for another second. He rose to his feet and set the controller down.

"Since that's the case, I'm going to go to bed," he said holding out his balled up fist.

Tae bumped it with hers and Jaelyn bypassed Syren, rolling his eyes at her in the process.

Syren had grown accustomed to Jaelyn's tantrums, backlash, and rebellious ways, yet after all these years, it still hurt Syren's feelings.

"Mama's baby, Daddy's maybe"… With Jaelyn, it was the other way around. He felt as if she was mean because she set rules that she expected him to follow, and he was disciplined when he did otherwise. However, Syren did it all out of love.

Slumped, she dragged into the kitchen. She could hear Tae on the phone with her chick. She knew the separation was killing them.

Angie was healing quicker than what she was expected. Early in the week, she picked up a second job to keep her busy. Sometimes Syren forgot she was there.

A sudden knock on the door startled her a bit because it was louder then usual.

"You're expecting someone?" Tae asked calmly.

"No, just your brother, and he has a key," she answered, walking past Tae and towards the door.

"Make sure it isn't the law before you open it," she whispered loudly. Her seemingly calm face had become panic-stricken.

Syren peeked out the window, instantly spotting Angie's husband Brandon. "Shit!" she called out, glancing at Tae.

"Who is it?" Tae asked.

"Angie's husband. I'll be back. I'm about to wake her up."
Syren ran down the hall to the room Angie was sleeping in.

"Angie. Angie!" she said, nudging her foot.

"Huh?" she mumbled, peering up at Syren through squinted eyes.

"Brandon down there beating on the door like he the——"
The loud commotion downstairs stopped her from speaking for an entire minute. She looked around stunned, mouth hanging open. Syren fled from Angie's room, making her way downstairs. Dressed in nothing but an oversized T-shirt, Angie followed close behind her.

"What you talm bout?" Tae asked, pulling up her Nike gym shorts.

"Tae, what the hell?" Syren asked, frightened.

"Nah, this nigga beating on the door like he bought this bitch. Fuck that, this my brother shit!" she responded, enraged.

"Angie! Angie!" Brandon called out, rubbernecking past Tae.

"What? Brandon, I'm done with you. I'm tired of you putting your hands on me."

"Come home, Angie, please? I miss you and I need you."

"No, you need help. I'm done."

"Angie, don't make me drag you out here."

"You're not going to lay a hand on her up in my house!"

"Be quiet, Syren! I ought to choke you out for letting her stay here."

"This my shit. I can——"

"Say, bruh, you done went too far. Just get the fuck out. Straight up."

"Bitch, you ain't"——

Tae hit Brandon with a left jab and right hook, stunning him. The two swift licks made his head jerk, but he shook it off effortlessly.

"Oh, bitch, you think you a man?" Brandon whispered, posted in his fighting stance.

Brandon was at least three inches taller and 100 pounds heavier than Tae, but it didn't frighten her a bit. They exchanged blows, but after Brandon connected a few of the haymakers, you could see the toll it was taking on Tae. Syren quickly scanned the room, spotting the iron. She grabbed it using the cord. She tossed it from behind around his neck, yanking the cord to secure it. She jerked harder, slowing his movements, allowing Tae to get the best of him. Syren used the cord to control his movement as she backpedaled out of her home. Realizing Tae was no longer his priority, Brandon stopped swinging and tried reaching for the cord. Once they were completely outside, Syren dropped the cord and flew past him into the house. Tae was bent over in the front room trying to catch her breath.

"Bitch-ass nigga!" Tae yelled before slamming the door shut.

Angie remained motionless on the couch, her eyes wide, evidence that she was still in shock. Out of the blue, something dawned on Syren, forcing tears into her eyes.

"What's wrong with you?" Tae asked, completely confused, still heavily breathing.

"I'm getting so sick of your fucking brother. What if you hadn't been here? That could've gone left. I could've got the same ass whooping he gives Angie and she could've got beaten all over again," Syren ranted.

"All that matters is I'm here. Don't worry about the if's. Go back to bed, Angie. I'll be back. I'm going to check on Jaelyn," Tae voiced, heading to Jaelyn's room.

"Angie?"

"Huh?" she answered, still in a trance.

"I apologize for——"

"Don't apologize. He's been beating my ass for years. He needs his ass beat. What I am going to do is get me a room tomorrow until I can find my own place. I don't feel comfortable bringing drama to your doorstep," Angie assured before walking off.

"But Angie, you——"

"No. You've been nothing but a friend to me. I know you don't mind helping, but I'm good, Syren."

With that, Syren remained quiet. Angie's mind was made up. She flopped down on her sofa, exhausted. It had been a minute since she'd been that physical. She knew eventually he would come. She was just glad it wasn't a night she and Angie was alone.

"He's good. Still sleeping. Apparently he fell asleep with his Beats on listening to the music on his iPad."

"Okay, great." Syren sighed, relieved.

"I know that dude's face from somewhere. I just can't remember."

"You sure?" Syren asked, turning around to face her.

"Yeah. Matter of fact, he's a resident in Maine's apartment complex."

"Nah, him and Angie own their home. That's where he at now, while she's here," Syren stated, troubled by her accusation.

"I'm positive. Come to think of it, I just saw him bring Maine some money into the office a few days ago."

Syren couldn't believe what she was hearing. Why hadn't Maine told her, knowing what Angie was enduring?

"Aahh." Tae winced, gripping her shoulder.

"You good, Tae?" she asked, concerned.

"My shoulder. I must've popped it out of place again. I did it years ago playing basketball. I know how to pop it back in. It's just too sore right now," she admitted.

"Hold on." Syren jumped to her feet, grabbing a towel from the pantry. She dashed into the kitchen, retrieving ice. She placed a handful of ice into the towel and placed it on Tae's shoulder.

"Ooooh," Tae moaned. There was even a small knot where her edge up began.

"Tae, you know you got a knot, right?" she asked while lightly pressing it.

"For real?" she inquired, peering up at Syren. "I got it," she said, grabbing the towel from Syren. "I still dropped that nigga huh?"

"Hell yeah," Syren agreed, stroking her ego. Tae did truly hold her own for Brandon to be his size.

The sound of keys jingling ceased Syren's movement and her heartbeat sped up in anticipation. Maine walked in with the cheesiest expression, angering Syren even more. Seeing both Tae and Syren's expressions, his smile slowly vanished.

"What——"

"Where have you been?" Syren expressed with an attitude, cutting him short.

"Me and Dekari were at the gambling shack. I thought I told you this."

"No, you didn't tell me, but whatever, Jermaine."

"What's up, Tae? What happened? You alright?"

"Yeah, I'm——" Tae started.

"She had a fight with Angie's husband. If you would've been here, you could've handled it."

"That fool hurt any of y'all? It's cool. I got his bitch ass, on me," Maine expressed, patting his chest.

"Do he have an apartment in the Falls, Jermaine?"

"Why you say that?" He scowled, offended.

"Well, I figured he did when I saw him bringin' you money last week," Tae chimed in.

"As a matter of fact, he do have an apartment in the Falls."

"For what? When he shares a house wit' Angie?"

"That's not my business, Syren. I'm just a businessman."

"Thats not right, Maine. You could've at least told me," Syren argued.

"You don't need to know that"

"Just like she don't need to know you fucking Uh'Nija?" Angie intervened.

"What you say, Angie?" Syren asked through narrowly slitted eyes.

"He's fucking Uh'Nija, Syren!" she yelled.

"That's a lie! Get out of my house. Get the fuck out! Ain't no bitch coming in between me and mines!" Maine yelled.

"She's not——"

"Oh, so now I don't have a say so in my shit?" Syren peered at Angie before lowering her head.

"You don't have to tell me twice. Nigga, my shit already packed."

"How do you know this Angie?" Syren yelled out in desperation. She just needed to hear anything, something. The truth, even lies, just something to secure her momentarily. On the inside she wanted Angie to admit it was a joke, but when the words left from her lips, Syren's womanly intuition told her it was the truth.

It's hard being strong when you don't have the strength.

"The night someone threw that brick into your salon. He was out fucking her. He mistakenly stayed longer than he planned and needed an alibi. A damn good one too. So he got Dekari to throw the brick inside. He couldn't chance you waking up and seeing his side of the bed empty. I overheard him talking to Dekari about it one morning after you left to take Jaelyn to school," Angie admitted.

"That's a lie, Syren! I wouldn't dare do no ho' shit like that. While you worried about me, you need to worry 'bout that husband of yours running through the money in y'all savings just to rent out a vacant to fuck that boy."

Everyone gasped besides Maine. Syren avoided eye contact with Angie and peered at Tae in disbelief instead. Without a word, Angie retreated towards the rear of her house.

"Maine, I think you should leave for the night. I need time to think about some things," Syren suggested.

"For real, Syren?" he inquired

"Dead ass."

"Cause of this bitch's lies?" he asked, looking appalled by her decision.

"Just respect my mind and get out, bruh."

"Bruh? Oh, you gangsta now?"

"Oh, you didn't know I was a savage?" she questioned.

Maine erupted with laughter, leaning against the doorway. Angie appeared moments later with her suitcase and MK duffle bag. Tae grabbed her things and walked them to the car.

"I love you. I'll text you once I'm settled and I'll give you a call in the morning. Don't trip. It's time we give they ass a taste of their own medicine," Angie whispered, releasing both of her arms she had wrapped around Syren.

Maine mumbled something once Angie bypassed him and she responded, matching his tone, before walking out.

Syren shot Maine one of those "What you waiting on?" glances. He walked out mere moments after Angie. Syren dashed to the window to assure he wasn't trying to harm Angie, but Angie had already disappeared. Maine glared at Syren before peeling off. She then glanced over at Tae, who nursed her shoulder. She simply lowered her head once their eyes met.

Syren headed to her bedroom, peeking in on Jaelyn, who was still sound asleep. Tears formed in her eyes, falling the closer she got to Jaelyn. She bent down and softly pecked his forehead before leaving. The last thing she wanted was to divide their family, but if there was any truth in Angie's accusation, she would do so in a heartbeat.

Syren removed her clothes and slid into the shower. She cried so hard she thought she would run out of tears. "Why, Lord?" she asked, staring up at the ceiling. Her heart ached so harshly. She clutched it to try and ease the pain. She used the water to rid herself of the tears and snot that fell rapidly.

Syren turned the water off and climbed out of the tub, using a gold clip to pin her bundles up. She hydrated her skin with Burt Bees intense day lotion before throwing on her silk robe. She scrolled through the iPod, pressing H.E.R. playlist before laying across the bed. She was trying to fall asleep when Tae walked in.

"Hey, I think Angie just texted or maybe called you," she said, holding up Syren's phone."

"Oh okay, I forgot all about that." She quickly sat up, reaching for her phone, not realizing her robe wasn't tied and revealing all her goodies. She didn't notice until Tae glanced down at her neatly-shaved vagina, compelling her to follow her eyes. She quickly tied her robe before standing to her feet.

"I'm sorry," she apologized.

"You good," Tae voiced, handing her the phone then turning to walk out.

"Tae!" she called out as her lips began to tremble.

"Huh?"

"I know you don't like me and have never liked me, but can you please just hold me? Please?" she begged.

Tae shook her head knowing she couldn't follow up on the request, but she felt so bad for Syren. Although she disliked her, she didn't deserve what she was being put through.

"Come on, Syren, you know I can't do that."

"Why not?"

Syren inched closer, so close Tae could feel and smell her breath. Her vanilla shampoo lingered around Tae's nostrils, instantly causing her clit to thump. They stared at one another for what felt like an eternity. Tae wanted to leave her standing there so badly, but lacked the control to do so.

Boldly, Syren leaned in and kissed her lips. Completely stunned at her sudden reaction, Tae quickly and desperately kissed her back. Their tongues danced as they explored every inch of each other's mouths. They swapped saliva like they'd known each other for years. Moans and grunts filled the room. Tae slurped on her tongue and sucked on her bottom lip while cupping her ass cheek. "Focus" by H.E.R. played, intensifying the already lit mood.

Syren removed her robe compelling Tae to tighten her lips to prevent the drool from seeping out after seeing her bare assets. Tae slid Syren's C-cup breast into her warm mouth, causing her chest to rise and fall as if she was struggling to breathe. She swirled her thick tongue around Syren's nipple while gazing into her eyes. Their hands intertwined as Tae showed her right breast the same amount of attention she had shown the left. As Tae left a trail of kisses down her stomach, Syren squirmed the closer she got to her lovebox. Although it was wrong, at the moment it felt better than right. Tae's lips were soft as butter. Syren couldn't wait to feel them on her other set.

Tae pecked the top of her pussy and Syren opened her legs spread-eagle. There was no more squirming, nor was there a mental battle. Right or wrong, she wanted it. Veins protuded from Syren's neck as she squeezed her pussy muscles together to withstand the anticipation. Before Syren reacted out of wantonness, she felt Tae's breath on her clit. She deeply gasped as if she had been waiting her whole life for this moment. Tae sucked and slurped on her like she had been waiting for the moment as well. She took each lip into her mouth before attacking her love button.

"Ooooh, Tae, oooh shit," she whispered, gently grabbing her head.

Tae swiftly flickered her tongue back and forth across her clit. Her body stiffened, then relaxed once she began to suck on her clit, suppressing her ability to speak. Just when she thought the feeling couldn't get any better, Tae slid two of her fingers inside her wetness. Her eyes rolled to the back of her head as she thrust her hips upward. Syren's grip tightened, making Tae pick up her pace, hitting all her spots.

"Oohh...sss! Ooohh, Tae!"

Tae felt compelled to switch her movements. Syren slowly but forcefully bucked and pumped as she felt the orgasm rising.

"Not yet," Tae mumbled, barely lifting up.

Through wide eyes, Syren gave her a look of death. "What you——"

"Shut up!" Tae cut her short, diving back in, but not where she left off. She slid her tongue inside her ass, startling Syren. The feeling was beyond pleasurable, magnified by Tae rubbing her clit while doing so. It was a feeling she hadn't felt in all of her years on earth.

"Uggghhh!" she yelped out in pure ecstasy. Cum, piss, water - whatever it may be that releases from your urethra when you've reached your peak - shot out, landing on the dresser, barely missing the TV. Syren covered her mouth in embarrassment. Maine had made her squirt a time or two, but it was nothing compared to tonight.

"Move your hand," Tae demanded, but Syren didn't. Tae reached up and shoved her hand out of the way and said, "There's nothing to be ashamed of. You a woman, and that's what pussy do."

Syren was taken aback by Tae's vulgar, blunt statement.

"I'll be back," Tae said, sliding out of the bed and putting on her gym shorts.

Guilt consumed Syren, but it was momentarily because as soon as Syren heard the water running, she peered around, confused.

Damn, she not going to invite me to shower with her? Syren thought. She lay on top of the sheets motionless in a pool of her juices, to weak to move and too afraid of rejection to voice her thoughts. The sight of Tae completely dressed, and the sound of running water made Syren shift uncomfortably as Tae walked towards her, holding her hand out.

"Come on," she said. Strands of her hair had come out of her braids, sticking out a bit, enhancing her rugged look. Her skin looked so smooth it made Syren want to taste it.

Tae led Syren to the bathroom, then cut the running water off. The tub was full of suds, just how she liked it. One leg at a time, Syren climbed inside, Tae holding onto her hand the entire time.

"Go ahead and bathe. I'm going to change those sheets."

Syren's mouth dropped. Completely startled, she lowered her head, careful not to reveal her expression. Syren took her time scrubbing every inch of her body. She climbed out and dried off without getting dressed. She climbed under the fresh linen before dozing off.

***

Doctor Samuels was sitting in her office at her desk, waiting for an answer. Two days had passed since the two beautiful ladies visited the clinic. She instantly took to Syren since she was in her shoes once upon a time. She knew Syren was the wife because of the identical last name. She felt guilty knowing the other woman was right there in the lobby with her. As badly as she wanted to speak up, she kept it professional, but her old street ways wanted to erupt and say "Fuck that nigga".

Her nose flared as she thought about Uh'Nija's scandalous ass. She prayed before placing the call, hoping it wouldn't bite her in the ass for discussing the confidential information. For two days it had weighed heavy on her heart and she refused to hold it in another second.

"Hello?" Syren answered, her voice was raspy as if she had just awakened out of a deep slumber.

"This is Dr. Samuels at the First Women's Clinic in Buckner."

"Yes ma'am." Syren leaned up against the headboard.

"Look Syren, what I am about to tell you I have no business doing so, but I'll die if I hold it in another minute.

"Die? Oh my God, what's going on, Dr. Samuels?"

"Look, the day you came and tested positive for chlamydia, so did another young lady, about five minutes after you left. I know for a fact she got the disease from your husband because when I asked her the name of her most recent sex partner, she said Jermaine Wiley."

Although Syren had already believed Angie, hearing the sickening news disturbed her spirits all over again.

"Okay, um, Dr.Samuels, I promise to keep this between us."

A sigh of relief escaped Dr. Samuel's mouth after hearing Syren's words of assurance.

***

Syren entered her salon like a woman on a mission. Uh'Nija peered up at her then peered back down, obviously unfazed by the owner's presence.

"What color would you like your extensions?" Uh'Nija asked the lady in the chair

"I want——"

"Hey, gather all your equipment," Syren told her.

"What?" Uh'Nija scowled, flicking her wrist at Syren as if she was a peasant.

"Everything you brought in here, that belongs to Uh'Nija...get it and get out," Syren demanded, pointing her finger in Uh'Nija's face.

"What's the problem?"

"Say, you got two seconds to start packing or I'm gon' hit you with something harder than the Corona," Syren threatened, inching closer. She was now face to face with the bitch she had considered a "friend".

"I don't want no smoke, Syren, you got it," she expressed, holding her hands up in surrender.

Although she portrayed like she didn't want any smoke, she never put space between herself and Syren. Their nipples kissed as both ladies stood glaring into each other's eyes. Uh'Nija turned around and began gathering her things.

"Don't get bitter. Get better, bitch," Uh'Nija mumbled.

Syren's fist went crashing into Uh'Nija's jaw, snapping her neck. Kreesha ran from the back to see what the loud commotion was when she spotted Syren on Uh'Nija's ass.

"Syren, stop! Think about Jaelyn!"

"Fuck this bitch!" She grabbed Uh'Nija's hair, pinning her to the wall, limiting her movement. "Did you know she fucked Maine?" Syren asked Kreesha. Grunts escaped her mouth as she strained to keep her pinned

"She what? She what?" Kreesha asked, appearing appalled before jumping in. Kreesha punched Uh'Nija in the face, causing the back of her skull to ricochet off the wall.

"What the fuck?" the lady sitting in the chair hollered and then scrambled for the exit.

Uh'Nija swung back wildly, dropping her head in the process to avoid the stings from both Syren and Kreesha blows.

The tactic only worked for so long. Uh'Nija's head jerked upwards when Syren's left uppercut connected with her chin, causing her to stumble backwards.

"You trifling-ass bitch!" Syren yelled, charging Uh'Nija.

Syren tackled her down to the floor, pounding her face mercilessly, while Kreesha stood there cheering her on. Uh'Nija was no match for her. She used her arms as a barrier to prevent the blows from connecting, but it was flimsy and unsteady serving no purpose. Syren's fist colliding into Uh'Nija's face felt like freedom to a prisoner. She and Syren weren't best friends, but their bond was pretty solid - solid enough for Syren to to give her later extensions on her booth fee, to invite her to her home, discuss her personal business. They were pretty tight in Syren's eyes. Realizing she had beat Uh'Nija unconscious, she finally stopped swinging. She used Uh'Nija's shirt as a towel to remove the blood from her knuckles, then rose to her feet.

Chapter 11
Keep them squares out your circle

Maine sat behind the wheel of his Camaro, on his way to the office, completely surprised that Syren hadn't contacted him in any form. He didn't dwell on it too long, knowing that soon Syren would crack. The dick gave her withdrawals. "Like a prisoner needs commissary. She needs me. Before the sun sets, she'll be looking for me."

"What's up, boy?" Maine spoke into the phone.

"Where you at, nigga?"

"Building a fort."

"A fort?" Dekari questioned, taken aback.

"You lay enough wood, you can build a fort"

"You always playing. Hey, Kreesha just left about an hour ago talking out the side of her neck. You need to pull up."

"Bet."

Maine had just about had it with Kreesha's fat ass walking around making demands, but he had a huge awakening for her. Maine climbed out of the whip and marched into the office, ready to let Kreesha have it, but she wasn't anywhere in sight.

"Where she at?" Maine turned to Dekari

"I told you she was here an hour ago."

"She'll be back. You know Syren put me out last night. That bitch Angie was there, some things was said. Long story short, she exposed me and Uh'Nijas affair."

"Wait, so Syren knows about you and Uh'Nija?"

"Yep, broke her all the way down. I felt like shit, fool. You know me, I denied that shit to the end. I'm not never coming clean 'bout no shit like that and willing to hold my breath while taking the lie detector test. Whatever the hell it is that they do to throw off the test."

"Bruh, don't beat yourself up. Syren ain't no saint."

"What's that supposed to mean?"

"I'm just saying, ain't no bitch innocent or completely faithful."

"Bruh, you don't know Syren."

"Alright." Dekari might have been talking from experience, but in order to speak on all women, you had to have had them all.

"Uh-uh, nigga, you out of line, Maine!" Kreesha yelled, barging in.

"What's up, Kreesha, what's the problem now?"

"You said my rent for this month is covered, but I wake up to this late notice on my door," she said, tossing the paper into the air.

"Yeah, well, I changed my mind."

"Oh, so you want me to tell my cousin you fucking Uh'Nija?" she bluffed.

"Go ahead. She already knows."

"Whatever. We'll see," she said, waving Maine off while walking out of the office. She stopped abruptly and turned to face Maine. "I swear I can't stand your dirty dick ass."

"Dirty and all, you'll slob it down if I let you."

"Bitch, you crazy!" Kreesha shot back.

"Get the fuck out of my office, talking to me like I'm some peon, before you find an eviction notice on your door instead!"

Without a peep, Kreesha left the office.

***

"That's it, that's it right there," Maine mumbled, enjoying the lip service.

Maine's eyes rolled to the back of his head as his grip tightened on the back of Kreesha's. He was jerking it violently like he was shifting gears. Kreesha was sucking Maine like she was trying to win him from Syren. She was far from appealing to Maine, but he had something to prove. No favors, no bribe; just a sweet approach. He was a few seconds from releasing his semen down her throat. Truthfully, Kreesha had envied Maine and Syren's relationship in the beginning because he spoiled Syren, giving her any and everything she desired, while Kreesha struggled immensely and wore knock-offs.

"Eat that dick," he mumbled, thrusting upward.

Kreesha was going to work. She knelt down under his wooden desk. Dekari had left to make a run when Kreesha returned the phone call.

"I'm cumming, fuck!" Maine bit down on his lip so hard he nearly drew blood trying to prolong the outburst that was trying to come forth.

The warm liquid shot out and into Kreesha's mouth. Drops of semen hit the floor, forming a small puddle.

"Don't let another drop hit the floor," he spoke seriously through clenched teeth, peering down at Kreesha in disgust. "What the fuck?" he cursed loudly.

Kreesha choked on the creamy thick liquid that seeped out the corners of her mouth like an overflowing sink

"It's nasty, Maine, it's real salty," she commented with a sour expression.

"Bitch, how long you been sucking dick? This ain't none you never tasted before."

"Nah, it's something different," she argued.

Enraged, he pushed like a woman in labor. The sight of Kreesha alone made him sick and he wanted to degrade her to max. He kept pushing while the veins protruded from his neck, yet nothing came out.

"What, Maine?" she asked, looking pitiful.

"Open your mouth."

"Why?"

"Open your mouth, Kreesha."

As soon as her lips parted, he took aim and pissed towards the back of her throat, hoping to hit her tonsils. It lasted for merely three seconds before she closed her mouth. A little landed on her teeth before dripping onto her breasts. She used her hand to wipe her mouth, evidently agitated.

"Disgusting bastard, why would you do that?"

"Check this: jack me until I'm hard, suck me until I bust, and this time, just make sure you catch it, then you good to go."

"Hey, I need——" Syren busted in, but ceased her speech while squinting at Maine closely.

He jumped in fear. Syren was the last person he expected to pop up.

"Huh? What's up, baby?" Maine said, sitting up straight swiping the wrinkles out of his shirt.

"The fuck you doing?" she spoke in a low tone while inching closer.

"I'm just tired, bae, damn," Maine replied, pretending to yawn.

Syren walked up on Maine, peering under the desk. "Kreesha? For real, bitch? You and Uh'Nija? You the same bitch that helped me kick her ass yesterday. The fuck going on around here!" she hollered.

Maine thought she would lunge for Kreesha, but she lunged for him instead, punching him in the forehead. She clawed at his eyes, but Maine grabbed her roughly once he felt his lids and the skin under his eyes begin to burn.

"Let me go!" she yelled loudly as if he was kidnapping her.

Kreesha remained curled up underneath the table with both Syren and Maine blocking her way.

"I'll be coming for your trifling ass too. On my son! I got you, bitch!' she yelled, spotting Kreesha squirm from underneath the desk.

In all his years of dating Syren, Maine had never heard her speak so aggressively and recklessly. He couldn't bring himself to look into her eyes. She deserved to curse, scream, fight, and whatever else she need to do to feel better.

Syren struggled to free herself from his grip, but it was no use. Her strength was nothing compared to his. She used her knees to knee him in the side, but it was practically harmless. He let her knee and kick until she wore herself out. Kreesha flew from underneath the table and out the door without a single word spoken.

"I'm sorry, Syren, I am. I'm so sorry. I wasn't thinking, mama. The bitch offered me a drink. I believe she drugged me. Please hear me out," Maine pleaded, lowering his head.

"Let me go, Jermaine," she whispered.

"Okay, but don't swing on me, Syren."

"I'm done, bruh. You not even worth the fight, the time, let alone my energy."

With that being said, he released her arms.

Syren promptly spit in Maine's face. Maine pressed his lips tighter. He used the back of his hand to remove the spit while peering at Syren's backside on her way out the door.

"Fuck!" he yelled, slamming the palm of his hand down onto the desk.

***

"I'm chilling. You need some——" Tae lowered her phone mid-conversation when she spotted a distraught Syren.

Although she had been crying, she was still beautiful. Her shoulders sagged in defeat as she walked towards Tae.

"Bae, let me see what's up with Maine. Call me back," she mumbled into the receiver.

"What's going on?"

"Bae, Maine is in trouble. Call back in an hour," Tae voiced a tad bit louder.

"I love you."

"I love you too."

Tae slid the phone inside her pocket, rushing to Syren's side. Syren burst out in tears, leaning against Tae's chest. Tae wrapped her arms around her, squeezing her tightly. Syren whimpered and wailed hysterically. Tae's chest tightened as she sympathized for the beautiful woman who stood in front of her.

"Tell me what's wrong," Tae begged. Syren covered her face with her small but cute hands. "Come on, Syren."

"I walked in on Kreesha sucking his dick!" she yelled, jerking away from Tae, leaving her standing in the hallway.

Tae stood there motionless, undeniably appalled. She took off in Syren's direction, finding her on her bed curled up.

Tae eased the door shut behind her, then sat at the foot of her bed - the same bed they had shared the night before. A recap of last night's episode flashed through her mind and a sense of compassion and pity engulfed her. She reached out and grabbed ahold of Syren's foot to express assistance.

"He fucked my flesh and blood, Tae!" she yelled, her voice quivering.

Tae felt like she had to do something more drastic than massaging her feet. She eased up behind her, draping her arm around Syren's waist. She intertwined her hand with Syren's while they lay on top of the sheets, entwined like crabs.

Although Tae's heart was with Iesha, at the moment, she wanted to be there for Syren in more than one way.

"Syren?" she whispered.

"Huh?" she moaned, her head buried in the satin sheets.

"I got you," Tae promised.

It was as if her breathing ceased before Syren turned to face her. "What you say?" she inquired. Her eyes were bloodshot red and her lids were swollen.

"I got you. Never switch up on me," she repeated.

The pace of Syren's heart quickened as soon as the words left Tae's lips. Tae knew Syren had been through it the last few years and the last thing she wanted was to add to her pain.

"Nah, this between us. It can't go any further than where it went last night."

"What?" Tae positioned herself on her elbows.

"You're Maine's sister!"

"I don't give a fuck. I'm not scared of Maine. You continue to fear that nigga. You're going to be miserable for the rest of your life if you keep letting him control it."

Syren peered up at Tae through squinted eyes. Tae knew the smart comment would upset her, but someone had to tell her.

"I'm not scared of anything, but damn, where's the loyalty?"

"The loyalty!" Tae yelled through wide eyes, appalled by her question. Feeling herself on the verge of saying something she knew she'd regret, Tae climbed out of the bed, heading for the door.

"Dirty is macking something I don't and won't do. I can't knock how you feel. You're entitled to that. All I'm saying is, you should let me love you. Don't eat, sleep, and shit on the idea, 'cause you just might miss your opportunity," Tae announced before leaving.

Syren opened her mouth to call Tae back, but the words never left her mouth. Instead, she just lay on top of the cover as the tears poured down. Not only was she hurt, but now she was hurt and torn - torn in between two siblings. Last night with Tae was different, nothing like she'd ever experienced. It felt so amazing, so refreshing, mind-boggling, and profound. All this time Syren was under the impression that Tae hated her, yet she sexed Syren like she adored her, like she craved and desired her.

They had formed a connection, compelling Syren to feel as if they were on the same accord. During their lovemaking session, the two shared secrets, struggles, emotions, and carried burdens. Syren felt like she had known Tae her entire life. Although she could see herself with Tae, she knew it was going against everything she stood for and she wasn't ready for the drama that was yet to come.

***

Meanwhile, on the other side of town, moans and grunts along with the distinct odor of sex filled the spacious, fully furnished house. Kreesha and Chris lay on top of the plush carpet, entangled like a web. The sound of loud smacks sounded throughout the room. With each thrust, Chris gave Kreesha a hard pop to her backside. After a little thought, a broken heart, a couple of drinks, and a hot pussy. Kreesha finally decided to give in and agree to do things Chris's way, although it wasn't as simple as she thought it would be. Chris made her promise to pay at least half the amount of the damage she caused to his car. It was obvious he wasn't leaving his wife of nine years, so she was ready to accept her role and move on. Chris's sex was like freedom to a man in prison who had been wrongfully convicted. Her eyes rolled to the back of her head as she threw it back, careful not to throw her back out.

The jingling of keys startled the both of them. Although Kreesha was 265 pounds, she moved like she was half her size. Uh'Nija had already put her on game about wearing clothes that could be easily removed and slipped into, days before she helped Syren kick her ass. She preferred a trench with nothing on underneath, but Kreesha decided to take more of an incognito route with the simple sundress – pantyless, of course. She quickly clamped her bra close and slid into the hot pink maxi dress. It was easy since the dress was a size too big. She never removed the gold MK sandals that exposed her neat and nude pedicure. Completely dressed in a matter of seconds, she snatched her gold clutch off the table. Inside were her car keys, minus the alarm pad and house keys. Just her single car key. She hopped over the pillow and dashed for the back door.

Chris never said a word. He was just focused on straightening up the mess they made and making sure Kreesha made it out without being noticed. Just as the back door opened, Chris's wife Ashley was coming in.

"Hey hun——" she said, but stopped once she began sniffing around the place she called home. "Why does it smell like sex in here?" she asked through squinted eyes. Without waiting for Chris to respond, she ran through their four bedroom home only to return seconds later. She peered around like a possessed woman.

Ashley had caught Chris cheating on her times before in the past, so anything he said in his defense fell on deaf ears. She had serious trust issues. She yanked open the front door. She looked for any unusual parked cars or if there were any cars speeding off towards the opposite direction, but the street was still and quiet.

She glanced to her left at her cheesy next door neighbor. "The fuck you smiling for?"

"'Cause I can. It's a free country."

"You fucking my husband?" she pried through squinted eyes, inching closer to the lady.

"There you go, Ashley," she voiced.

Chris stepped onto the porch to see what was going on. When he heard Ashley questioning the neighbor, he exhaled deeply, knowing Kreesha had gotten away.

"Come on, hunny, you're bugging. I would never have a woman in this house we share, let alone another woman period."

"Shut the hell up! Your dirty dick ass isn't any good." She bypassed him and went inside her home. She had no proof. She lowered her head and headed upstairs.

Chris was sweating like a slave, hoping that Kreesha had grabbed everything she owned. Any form of evidence that was left placing her at their home could destroy his marriage for ever.

In the meantime, Kreesha was hunched down in her metallic Nissan Altima, sweating like a Hebrew slave as the sun beams attacked her effortlessly. She sat still as a board, afraid to move. Nothing moved but the sweat that rolled down and through the crack of her ass. She was scared to cover her face with her palms to avoid the direct sunlight. She stayed alert just in case she got busted. Uh'Nija's words replayed in her mind as she peered out the side mirror.

"If she ever comes home and you have to make a run for it, just hop in and be still, because if she come out and sees a car pulling off, her assumption would be correct. Dress light, pack lighter, and be quick on your toes. Wait five to seven minutes, then pull off."

Kreesha looked down at her watch. She had exactly one minute left. When the time came, Kreesha eased up, glancing in the rearview mirror before peeling out.

Chapter 12
At the salon

Syren sang along to the lyrics while gathering all of Kreesha's things and cleaning up the mess from her and Uh'Nija's brawl the day before.

> "See you don't have to worry 'bout me
> You made it clear that you're unhappy
> So go ahead and have your fun now
> Just remember what goes around, comes around…"

The salon was empty. The closed sign hung out front for all her customers who enjoyed doing walk-ins. The sound of the doorbell forced her to jerk her head in the direction of the noise.

"Hey, we're closed——" Syren started, but stopped when she noticed the familiar face.

"I tried setting an appointment for my dreads, but the line up here is busy."

"You're Draco, Tae's friend, right?"

"Yeah, I came by with Tae the other day."

"Yes, I remember," she responded nervously. Remnants of blood could still be seen and she tried standing in front of the towel so Draco wouldn't notice it.

"I'm not the Feds, Syren, you can trust me"

"Yeah, right," she mumbled, tired of hearing the overused word that absolutely held no value to her, since the very person whose blood she just cleaned up used the same words and crossed her to the extreme.

"I don't have to convince you. I'm a woman of few words I let my actions speak for me," Draco said, bypassing Syren, grabbing the towel out of her hands and using it to clean up the remains of the fight.

"You ready?" Syren asked.

"You sure?"

"Yeah. I'm not about to let her fuck up what I have going on. Remove your shirt so I can toss it in the washer."

"My shirt?" Draco asked, dumbfounded.

"You ask a lot of questions. I don't want you leaving here sweaty. It won't take longer than your hair and besides, I have to wash mine, so why not?"

"Fuck it," Draco agreed, removing her YSL shirt. "Hey Syren!" she called out. Syren didn't bother to look up. Draco felt obliged to call her name again until she was giving her undivided attention. "Syren?"

"Huh?" she snapped.

"Hey, these are a little sweaty too," Draco said, clutching the crotch of her shorts.

Syren swallowed the lump in her throat, then said, "Okay, take them off too. She appeared calm, but Syren was truly ruffled watching Draco stand before her in just a red and black Reebok's sports bra along with a black pair of briefs. Her body was a masterpiece and her chiseled features were trulely a sight to see. The tattoo of an AK-47 on her stomach was fiya. "Show no love" was tatted in cursive underneath it.

"Syren!" she called.

Syren had been so mesmerized by her nudity that she forgot her manners and the task at hand.

"Oooh. I'm sorry. Give them to me." She ran off to the back, placing both hers and Draco clothes inside the washing machine. She slid on a pair of yoga pants and a crop top that she had put up in the cabinet for her pole dancing lessons.

"Oh, okay, you changed," Draco said, sitting comfortably in the leather chair.

156

"Yeah, well, I mean, I have plenty of stuff like this in the back you can wear," Syren suggested, smirking.

"Don't play with me, Syren," she shot back, straight faced.

"Okay, come on." Syren rushed behind her to begin twisting her hair.

"I'm fucking with you," Draco said, turning around to face her. Her smile was beautiful and inviting.

She had plenty of new growth. On top of that, she had a good grade of hair. Her dreads were shoulder-length and platinum blonde at the tips. The roots were sandy red.

The first few dreads Syren twisted in complete silence.

"So are you going to tell me why there was blood in your salon?" Draco asked.

Needing someone else to vent to, she broke down and told Draco everything, play by play. She spoke candidly. You would've thought she had known Draco for years.

"How do you know Uh'Nija?" she pried.

"We had a little thing going on, but——"

"It doesn't matter. I don't even know why I asked," Syren rudely chimed in. "Shit! Hold on," Syren voiced. She was so busy telling her everything that transpired that she forgot to put the clothes in the dryer. She quickly did so, returning to the front.

"Would you like something? I'm ordering from What-A-Burger," Draco said, covering the receiver on her phone.

"Here?" Syren asked.

"Yes. Are my clothes done?"

"No. Get me a patty melt and large onion ring. I don't want anything to drink. I have a mini fridge full of beverages in the back."

"Cool. I got you."

Syren was three dreads away from finishing when the door chimed. Draco jumped up to grab the food and tip the driver. The UberEats driver was a chick who stared at Draco lustfully. Draco offered her a tip and she declined it before winking and walking away. *Dumb bitch*, Syren thought.

Draco sat down as Syren reached in to finish her hair. Draco turned around to face her and said, "Let's eat. Do you have somewhere to be?" She gazed up into Syren's eyes.

Syren set everything down and sat in the chair closest to Draco. She didn't realize how hungry she was until the aroma from the food filled her nostrils. She wasted no time diving in. Syren ate so fast she wasn't able to talk in between bites

Draco snuck glances out of the corner of her eye. Honestly, she enjoyed seeing Syren eat her food. She hated stuck up females, the ones who picked at the food instead of eating.

They finished their meals. Conversation during the time was scant. Syren finished the three dreads before retrieving the clothes from the dryer, bumping directly into Draco after shutting the dryer.

"I thought you may have needed help," Draco said, invading Syren's personal space.

Syren took a step back, nervously placing her hair behind her ear. "No, but here you go." Syren shoved her in the chest with her shorts and shirt. She tried walking past Draco, but Draco wouldn't move.

"Where you going? You're not going to change?"

"No, I don't need to," she said, blitzing past Draco.

Draco returned to the front minutes later, fully dressed. Her fresh dreads enhanced her beauty. That and her swag enticed Syren, making it hard for her not to give in to her charm. Syren checked her phone, instantly seeing the missed calls.

"Can I get your number so I can call you personally to set my appointments?"

"Oh, you want to set appointments? That's it?"

"And maybe this."

Draco leaned in and pressed her lips against Syren's. At first, Syren was a bit reluctant, but she quickly yielded to the overpowering desire. Truthfully, Syren wanted to feel Draco's lips the moment she walked in. She felt like an insect in a spider web. The only way out was to press through, adapt. She kissed her back aggressive, but passionately. She was the insect trying to escape the web -the web of pain, despair, and treachery. She used Draco to help her escape it all, even if it was just for the moment. They stared each other down once they broke their kiss.

"We have to go," Syren uttered, lowering her head. She was ashamed to look in Draco's eyes after feeling the wave of guilt.

Draco flashed a boyish, grin following Syren out of the door, only to be met by a cheerful Tae, whose smile vanished immediately.

"What's up, fam, you like my hair?"

"Yeah, but didn't I tell you to stay away from my brother's bitch?" Tae inquired, mugging Draco venomously.

"Damn, I can't get my dreads tightened?" she responded, dumbfounded.

"Nigga, you know what you doing, dawg. But this my last time telling you to chill on that bullshit," Tae stated, scowling harshly at Syren before peeling off. The look she gave Syren sent chills down her arm.

Ah'Million

Chapter 13
In with the new. Out with the old

Maine sobbed like a baby as Dekari leaned against the door to the office. He felt sorry for his dear friend upon seeing him in such a gloomy state, but like all the times before this one, he had warned Maine. He had fucked over Syren so many times he lost count.

"What should I do, man?"

"The choice isn't yours, bruh. You fucked her cousin"

"I didn't fuck her. I let her suck my——"

"Look, I'm not the one you need to convince. It's all the same fuckery.

"You right."

"Maine, when women love, they love hard. They'll go to the moon for you, but when they tired and fed up, it's a wrap. It's like trying to make parole when you're a three time loser. Ain't shit shaking," Dekari expressed intensely.

Dekari was right and Maine knew it. He reached into his pocket and retrieved his phone to call Tae.

Tae peered down at her phone. Her charger was so smoky from the exquisite weed, she had to squint to make out the name on the screen.

"Here, it's Keith Sweat," Tae told Syren, handing her the phone.

"You funny." She spoke in between giggles.

"Why you call him that?"

"'Cause he begging right now as we speak."

Syren and Tae were chilling in the lot of the neighborhood park. Syren had a lot on her mind and needed to relieve some stress. She passed on the opportunity of visiting her mom, knowing she wouldn't take her seriously. She had mentioned leaving Maine numerous times before. Instead of telling her mother, Syren would just show her. Tae had been running the streets a lot lately. Honestly, she'd been skeptical about Syren and Draco since running into them at the salon. Her suspicion really rose when she noticed Syren's change in attire the day she found them at the salon.

She placed the tightly-rolled blunt in between her lips. taking a drag, blowing it into Tae's direction.

"That's why you don't get high!"

"Why?" she asked Tae, baffled.

"You doing it wrong. Let me see." Tae grabbed the blunt and inhaled deeply. "You can't just blow the smoke out. You have to inhale that shit," Tae commented, passing her the blunt back.

Syren did exactly as instructed. Before long, she was coughing, coughing so hard that tears formed in her eyes. Tae quickly grabbed the blunt while patting her in the back.

"Damn, girl, you coughing and spreading germs like this pandemic not occurring."

Syren held up her middle finger while doing breathing exercises to cease the cough.

"Aww, that baby crying," Tae teased, looking at Syren, who was dabbing the tears out the corner of her eyes. She poked her lips out and leaned towards Tae. "Nope," Tae declined.

"For real, Tae?" Syren asked, surprised that Tae wouldn't give her a kiss.

"Yeah. We don't have any kind of understanding. You not about to keep taking dick and I'm fucking you. You gon' choose or lose, straight up."

"You think I'm going back to that?" she asked in shock.

"I don't know what you gon' do. Bitches are ignorant."

"That's your perception of me?" she asked, turning towards the window.

162

"No, it's not, Syren. I think highly of you. I liked you so much I hated you because you weren't mine."

Syren slowly turned to face Tae after hearing her admit what she already knew. She knew Tae hated her, but she never understood why.

She climbed over the seat and straddled Tae. Their lips collided as they explored each other's mouths as if it was a moment they had long awaited. After the passionate kiss, Syren slid into the passenger seat as Tae drove off. Tae bent the corner, spotting Maine's car in the driveway.

"Oooh shit!" Syren cursed, looking into Tae's direction.

"What are we going to say?" Syren continued.

"Out of respect, 'cause he's my brother, I'll go along with your lie, but I'm not going to keep lying."

Tae pulled alongside the curb. Maine hopped out shortly and so did Syren.

"I been calling the both of y'all," Maine spoke with urgency.

"I was busy," Tae shot back nonchalantly.

"My car wouldn't start, so I called Tae," Syren lied.

"Why didn't you call me?" he asked, seeming confused.

"Maine, I'm done with you!" Syren screamed.

"But Sy——"

"But what? Do you really think I'm going to take you back after fucking my cousin? Kreesha was like a sister to me! You knew that."

Maine lowered his head in embarrassment. He felt like shit. "I'm so sorry, baby. I'll do anything, anything, to make it like it was. I promise to give you my all and nothing less. Just give me another chance to make it right," he begged as the tears fell from his eyes.

Surprisingly, Syren didn't feel a hint of sympathy. She simply looked at him in disgust and walked past him.

Tae was waiting on the steps. She unlocked the door and Tae closed it.

"Syren!" Maine yelled from the other side of the door. She'd forgiven him too many times before and he assumed it would work again.

"Not this time. I'm making a believer out of his ass. Remind me to change the locks first thing in the morning," she told Tae, tossing the keys on the counter.

***

"Granny, when will our house be fixed?" Jaelyn asked, shooting the ball into the hoop above the garage.

"You know better than I do," Shelia mumbled.

"Huh?"

"Oh, baby, I said it should be soon, very soon. You ready to leave your big momma?"

"No ma'am. I just miss spending time with Mom, Dad and Aunty Tae," he admitted.

Sheila had been dropping off and picking up Jaelyn for the past three days. She honestly felt that Syren would just take Maine back. He would just pay his way back in like he did every other time. It didn't bother Sheila whatsoever as long as it wasn't affecting her grandson. She actually enjoyed Jaelyn's company since she stayed alone. Sheila was a beautiful older woman, yet she was single because her expectations were too high.

"You hungry, J?"

"Yes ma'am," he responded while Sheila stood to her feet. "What you gon' make, Granny?" he asked.

"A pressed ham sandwich with chips."

"That's alright," he mumbled, lowering his head. He continued to shoot hoops.

"Your ass not hungry then."

It was the only thing Jaelyn disliked about Grandma's house. There were rules, sometimes to many.

A couple of blocks from Sheila's house, Draco and Tae staked outside the Gold's Gym, looking for the perfect candidate.

"If nothing shakes in minutes, we going to head to Bally's in Duncanville," Draco insisted.

"Bet, 'cause I got some shit to handle," Tae said, peering sharply around the lot.

"I saw your in-law at the bank. She looked a little stressed," Draco mentioned in an attempt to gain information.

"Yeah, her and my bro split."

"So is it a problem if I shoot my shot?" Draco asked, glancing at Tae.

"Hell yeah! He's not done, so you know how that shit go. It's a galore of bitches. FInd you one. She's off limits, plain and simple," Tae stated. She was sick of Draco inquiring about Syren. Right then she knew she had to grind day in and day out because as soon as Draco got wind off her and Syren, Tae was certain Draco would be salty and cut her off. They had a nice gig going between herself, Draco, and Tangy.

Draco was excited to hear the split was definite. Now all she has to do was find her way into her presence. She and Tae were cool and all, but if hooking up with Syren meant jeopardizing that, then so be it.

"Besides, she's not even gay," Tae added, a little salty.

"Bruh, come on. You been fucking with females long enough to know every female isn't gay, but all of them are curious. Every straight chick I done had hit me with the same line right before I hit her with the nine, nine times. I can have any bitch I want. They all gay in my eyes," Draco voiced arrogantly.

"Yeah, you right. Hey, that's it right there, huh?" Tae pointed at the Caucasian lady slamming the door on her Cadillac CTS.

"Yep. Come on." In unison, Tae and Draco stepped out of the black Chevy Malibu.

The petite Caucasian lady opened the door to the gym while Draco and Tae dashed discreetly to her car. She drove a newer model CTS. Cranberry paint job, peanut butter interior. As they eased across the street, they both listened attentively for the sound of her alarm, but it never sounded.

Draco peered to the left, then right, before lifting the handle on the driver's side door. Once it opened, she eyed Tae, smiling mischievously. Tae sat on the trunk of the CTS and put fire to the Newport to look comfortable rather than suspicious. She pulled her cap down just in case cameras were nearby. After Draco closed the door, they strolled back to the Malibu without being noticed.

Damn, I thought Iggy was fine, Tae thought, staring at the thick blonde that made her way to the car. Everything sat pretty and appeared well-proportioned. She was exactly how Draco described her: bad.

The pencil shirt hugged her body tighter than a latex glove. The white V-neck crop top exposed her cleavage. Normally Tangy stood 5' 3", but the multi-colored wedge heels gave her at least four more inches.

"What's up, boo? How you doing?" she greeted, speaking to Draco, then Tae.

"Chillin'," they responded in unison.

"I need you to handle this for me. Shoot me a text and let me know what she got going on."

"Anything for you, boo," she replied, tucking the pocket-sized Ziplock bag inside of her bra.

She strutted off immediately. Her ass didn't jiggle, so Tae assumed she has a little work done, which didn't faze her any. Fake or not, the girl still looked appeasing.

"Give me an hour!" she turned around and called out.

***

"Hey Mom, can I please come home?" Jaelyn asked, climbing into the vehicle.

Sheila had planned on picking Jaelyn up like she had done so the past three days, but Syren phoned her today with a change of plans. She missed Jaelyn. The phone calls weren't enough for her. She was sick of Jaelyn cutting their conversations short just so he could play his video game or listen to music. According to the way he treated her, Syren honestly believed he was enjoying the time away at his grandmother's. She was shocked to hear him ask such a question.

"Sure, baby. The house is almost finished anyways." She hated lying to Jaelyn, but she didn't want to tell Jaelyn the truth, knowing it would expose Maine's disloyalty and take away from his character. She would never want to disappoint Jaelyn when he worshipped the ground his father walked on.

Jaelyn tried concealing his excitement, but she spotted his pearly whites before it was too late.

The rest of the ride home was short and quiet when it came to Syren. Jaelyn was never really talkative. Something about his mother made his ass itch.

"Oooh, Aunty Tae!" Jaelyn yelled, spotting Tae's car in the driveway.

Jaelyn's reaction made her smile, knowing Tae made the both of them fall in love with her in just a matter of days.

"You love Aunty Tae? Huh?" she asked sarcastically, never taking her eyes off the road.

"Yes, Momma. Aunty Tae plays video games with me, buys me shoes, tells me about girls, and visits me sometimes at practice."

"About girls?" she pried.

"Momma, I don't want to talk about that with you. That's why I asked her," Jaelyn responded.

"You right. I never knew Tae visited you at practice," she said, surprised but impressed.

Jaelyn hopped out before she came to a complete stop. She started to yell, but she shook her head instead. Syren followed Jaelyn inside. Tae and Jaelyn stood in the doorway hugging when she bent the corner. She could feel the butterflies in the pit of her stomach as soon as she and Tae made eye contact. Afraid, Jaelyn could somehow read their mind, she lowered her head and rushed inside.

"Go put ya stuff up, li'l man. Shower so you can be fresh like me, and then I'm gon' kick yo ass on this 2k."

"Okay," Jaelyn said, rushing down the hallway.

Tae eased up on Syren in the kitchen after realizing they were alone.

"Hey, go look on your bed. I got you something." Without responding, she took off, grabbing Syren by the hand, pulling her back, invading her personal space.

"Give me a kiss first," she requested, licking her thick and succulent lips.

Syren peered around quickly to make sure Jaelyn wasn't around, then leaned in and planted a slow and passionate kiss on Tae's lips. The kiss alone dampened her pussy.

She playfully broke away from Tae's embrace and rushed to her bedroom. The massive Louis Vuitton duffle bag stood out amongst everything else. She gasped and her eyes grew twice their size. Picking up the bag, placing it on her shoulder, she walked to the full-length mirror to stare at her reflection. "Thanks Tae," she whispered.

Inching closer towards her, Tae backpedaled, sticking her head into the hall for sounds of Jaelyn nearing. "He in the shower," Tae said, smiling mischievously.

Together they leaned in. Their lips instantly collided and moans and grunts filled the room. Slowly but lustfully, they used their tongues to curb the flaming desire and irresistible urge they contained for one another.

"Jaelyn," Syren whispered.

Immediately, Tae pulled back at the sound of his name.

"Look, I'm going to go check on Angie. I'll be back. I haven't seen her since the big fight and I need to see my friend."

"Cool. I'm about to get on this 2k with Jaelyn's bad ass."

Syren put the mini MK bag inside of the duffel bag and placed it on her arm so she could show her expensive gift to Angie. Angie was her only friend left. She was still staying in the hotel, so they decided to meet at Applebees.

***

Syren's and Angie's champagne glasses clinked as they sat at the table, enjoying each other's company. Angie's appearance had already changed in the few days away. She always dressed so conservatively - but not tonight. The mini red dress she wore accentuated her brown skin. The waist trainer hid her stomach and enhanced her ass. She was glowing like a woman carrying her seed. Her peanut butter brown wedges matched her Prada bag.

"I like that purse, girl. You going shopping crazy to fill that void?" Angie asked, eyeing Syren's bag.

"No. It was a gift from a relative."

"Damn, my people don't even call and wish me a happy birthday. My aunt will, but after she tells me happy birthday. she asks me for money. Now when she calls, I don't answer."

They shared a laugh before taking another sip.

"You look great. Have you seen or heard from Brandon?" Syren asked, looking over the rim of the glass at Angie.

"No, but I get a thousand texts a day. I find it hard to believe that he's willingly giving me space."

"Let me know if he decides to pull up with that bullshit. Me and Tae going to get to you at record speed," Syren stated seriously.

Angie stared at her, left brow raised.

"What?" Syren questioned, breaking the silence.

"Look, Syren, I'm just going to come out and say this because you are my friend and I love you genuinely."

"Okay," Syren said, swallowing the lump in her throat.

"People are going to talk regardless. You can do everything right and they'll still find something wrong. I'm saying, fuck the people. Do whatever it is that makes Syren happy. In the end, you have to answer. Can't no one answer for you. Life is all about happiness - love and happiness, to be exact."

Syren nodded her head in agreement then asked, "Where did this come from?"

"I heard you and Tae fucking."

Syren gasped as soon as the words escaped Angie's mouth. Her heart raced as she began to wonder if anyone else heard them.

"I left my wallet and I also forgot to give you back the extra key you had made for me, so I let myself in and grabbed what I needed. I thought you were up there with Maine, which upset me, until I heard you call out Tae's name. It was definitely unexpected, but I shrugged it off and kept it moving. What you doing is the same shit he done to you. Fuck him."

"Well, since you know, bitch, let me tell you the rest…"

Ah'Million

Chapter 14
It's too late to apologize

Maine sloppily sat on the stool at the bar. Dekari sat next to him. Dekari had become slightly irritated with the late calls and random pop-ups, but he couldn't mention that to his longtime friend. Although he knew this day would come, saying "I told you so" wouldn't lift his spirits. He truly felt sorry for Maine. It's proven that when a man gets caught cheating, it affects him within. They feel as if they're supposed to do anything but get caught.

"What should I do, man?" Maine pleaded through sorrowful eyes.

"She's highly upset. Bruh, you did the unthinkable. You're going to have to give her some time."

"How much time?"

"Enough. Until she gets ready. It's not about you. It's about her."

Feeling defeated, Maine staggered to his feet. "Take me home, bruh."

Dekari stood, and placing Maine's arm across his shoulder, he led him out of the bar.

Maine decided to shack up in one of the vacant units in the apartments. He hadn't spoken to Uh'Nija much in an attempt to do the right thing.

Maine was knocked out cold by the time they made it to the Falls. Taking care of someone with a broken heart was like caring for an elderly or child. It was a huge responsibility.

"Maine! Maine! Maine!" Dekari repeated, startling him.

"Huh?" he answered, quickly peering around.

"We here, come on," Dekari announced, unbuckling his seatbelt. He helped Maine out of the car and up the stairs.

"Look, man, straighten up before you fuck around and make both of us fall."

One at a time, they climbed the steps. Dekari used his left hand to hold onto the rail as they carefully made their way up. He reached into Maine's pocket and retrieved the keys. As soon as he unlocked the door, Maine stepped inside. Losing his footing, he fell to his side.

Dekari had run out of patience. He left him lying on the floor. He threw Maine's keys on the sofa, locked the bottom lock from the inside, and closed the door.

Dekari flew down the steps and into his car. Thinking of his next move, he turned the volume up and scrolled through his DM when he happened to peer up and spot Uh'Nija climbing the steps two at a time. Dekari shook his head in disgust. With everything occurring, Maine still hadn't learned. Seeing that vexed Dekari's spirit and without waiting another second he peeled off.

***

Syren leaned against the headboard while Tae lay between her legs, watching the show *The World of Dance*. Yesterday, Syren had confessed her feelings for Tae. She even agreed to start something, something she believed she'd regret, but for now, it was what she wanted. She'd worry about tomorrow when that day came. Tae made her feel special, loved, different, and youthful.

After dropping off Jaelyn at Maine's mother's this morning, they'd had the times of their lives. Wild sex throughout the house, Netflix, eating junk, but mainly enjoying each other's presence. Tae had a wonderful sense of humor and a few of her jokes nearly bought Syren to tears.

The ringing of Tae's phone diverted their attention.

"Hold on, bae," she told Syren before answering the phone "Hey mama, you good?" Tae asked.

Syren turned her attention back to the TV, knowing she wouldn't be on the phone with her mother long.

"I miss you too. Did you get the money I sent?" Tae asked, easing off the bed. "I'll send them tonight. I want to come see you," Tae voiced walking out the bedroom.

Syren finally realized it was her jail bitch. *As soon as she gets done, I'm going to set her ass straight*, she thought.Syren flipped through the channels, but watching TV was the last thing on her mind.

Tae returned smiling, closing the door behind herself. "What's wrong, bae?" she asked, pretending to not know the reason behind Syren's mug.

"Since there's no Maine, there is no Iesha."

"What?" Tae asked, appalled.

"I'm serious."

"Bruh, she's in prison on an eight year sentence. Why you tripping?"

"I'm tripping because I can."

"No you can't, and you ain't."

"Tae, listen——" Syren began.

Tae pressed her lips against Syren's to stop her from speaking. Syren folded her lips inside her mouth, but that didn't stop Tae from kissing her in other places. She wanted to resist, but her soft juicy lips against her flesh made her heart skip a beat and aroused her sexual desires. She was turned on even more as Tae peered into her eyes while planting the kisses

Knock! Knock! Knock!

"Oh my God, I think that's Maine!" Syren sat straight up in the bed.

"Today is the day I'm telling him," Tae announced, sliding out of the bed.

"You can't do that," Syren protested, straightening up the room.

"Who's going to stop me? I'm grown. I'm done creeping. He gon' either kill me or deal with me. I knew what it was when I decided to ease ya mind and penetrate your soul"

"Tae, I——"

"Police! Open up!"

"What the fuck?" they both whispered at once, peering at each other in disbelief.

Afraid, Syren rushed to the door with Tae on her heels.

"Wait," Tae whispered

"What?"

"I'm about to hide. More than likely, they looking for me."

"Okay," Syren said, giving Tae a few extra seconds to hide. She finally unlocked the locks, opening the door.

Three police officers stood at the door. One held a pair of cuffs.

"How may I help you, sir?"

"Are you Syren Wiley?"

Her mouth fell open and she stiffened. "Yes sir."

"You are under the arrest for assaulting Uh'Nija Smith on October 12th, 2020."

***

The metal bench was unlike anything Syren ever felt as she lay curled up on top of it. There was only one other person in the cell with her. She sat on the toilet, experiencing unbearable meth withdrawal. Tears slid inside Syren's ears, irritating her eardrums as she lay on her side, crying a river. Not once did she think kicking Uh'Nija's ass would come back to haunt her. In Syren's eyes, Uh'Nija owed her. She deserved that, and there shouldn't have been any consequences or repercussions.

"Ms. Wiley, let's go. You're being released," the white male officer announced.

Syren scurried to her feet, wiping the debris off her clothes. She knew it wouldn't take long for her bond to be posted since Tae was there and heard everything that occurred. She followed the guy down the long hallway, where she stopped in front of a desk and signed a few papers. Afterwards, she was led to a different desk that separated her from the clerk with a window made of plexiglass.

"What's your name?" he asked without looking up from the computer.

"Syren Wiley," she spoke proudly.

"Whaattt, the stylist behind bars?" she asked sarcastically, peering at Syren over the rim of her off-brand glasses.

"Can you run me my shit?" Syren asked aggressively.

"What?"

"You heard me. I'm free. I didn't come here to talk to you. Unlike myself, I don't know you. I just want what's mine so I can go open my salon."

The lady rolled her eyes, then slid Syren's cell phone inside the box. She snatched the box, retrieved her phone, then threw her bundles over her shoulder before strutting out of the jail. Any other time she would've enjoyed the breeze and beautiful sunset, but after spending hours in the uncomfortable cell, she just wanted to return home and shower.

Honk! Honk!

Syren squinted at the unfamiliar car parked directly in front of her. Hesitant, Syren didn't even budge; she stared in the direction of the car. Draco climbed out with a huge grin on her face.

"Come on, girl!" she yelled, signaling for Syren to get in.

Syren walked slowly to the car with a look of confusion and concern plastered across her face. Draco was the last person Syren expected to see.

"Damn, why you muggin'? I don't get a thank you after dropping twenty-five hundred on your bond?"

"You bonded me out?" Syren asked, shocked, while climbing inside the car. "Why? How did you even know?" she continued, completely puzzled.

"Well, I was on my way over to drop something off to Tae when I saw them putting you in the car. Instead of stopping, I followed the police cruiser, waited until you were in the system, then posted your bond.

"Oh, okay. Thanks," Syren responded skeptically.

"You good."

"No…thanks again. I got you."

"Hey, I know I have to respect your relationship, so to avoid the drama, just tell them it was one of your girlfriends," Draco said, hoping to receive some sort of information on her and Maine's status.

"You're right" she responded. Little did Draco know, Maine wasn't the first person she was worried about finding out. Besides, he shouldn't have any knowledge of her arrest unless Uh'Nija told him. Tae was the only one she was afraid of.

Draco didn't really want Tae to find out either - not this way, anyway. Especially after warning her to stay away. Syren was the woman Draco had been searching for, for a long time: a black, beautiful, strong and independent woman. Although Syren had her by seven years, age was merely a number.

"So, Ms. Syren…"

"Syren," she corrected.

"Okay, Syren. Can I have just thirty minutes of your time?"

"Okay. How will we kill this thirty minutes?" Syren questioned

"At a nice little restaurant."

"Dray, honest——"

"Draco."

"Draco, honestly, I'm not feeling any public places. I look a mess. And I don't smell too great either."

"I can't smell you - just a little breath, but no ass. You good. Just put your mask on.

Syren's eyes bucked in shock at Draco's blunt comment.

"Don't look at me like that, Syren, I'm just being honest. You been in a cell for hours."

"I'm grown. There's no need for an explanation," Syren chimed in.

"Okay. Is it cool if we stop at Baskin Robbins for some ice cream and take a stroll around the park?"

"Um…"

"You know what? I got you," Draco said, speeding up, as she headed to the Baskin Robbins. She turned up the volume up on Road Waves latest mixtape.

Syren pretended to be unfazed by the lyrics, but Draco could tell she wanted to bop to the beat.

"Okay, I'll go order since you don't want to be seen with a nigga."

"That's not the case, Draco."

"What kind you want?" she asked, changing the topic.

"I want a chocolate cone, three flavors: butter pecan, pistachio almond and Bridescake. In that order."

"Bet."

Draco strolled inside and ordered the ice cream. She got herself the same thing. She was familiar with the flavors Syren chose, except Bridecake. She was anxious to try it.

The Hispanic chick behind the counter lustfully eyed her from the time she walked in until she paid for the order. She was dressed plainly in a pair of navy blue and white Ralph Lauren joggers, white crisp V-neck with the small navy blue polo symbol, white briefs, and a pair of white Reebok classics.

When she headed for the exit, the chick said, "Hey, if you not seeing anyone, can I put my number in your phone?"

Draco flashed a grin, then replied, "I'm taken."

As she pushed the door open, she thought, *She don't know it, but she already mines.* Draco smiled at Syren as she approached the car. The park was just down the street. She parked in the small lot and opened the door. Reclining her seat, Draco placed one leg outside the vehicle. The beat to the song came on, making Draco stomach flutter. It was perfect timing. So many times prior to today made Draco think of Syren while listening to this song.

"Hey, this song reminds me of you, beautiful," she said, increasing the volume.

> *I know you not no good for me*
> *But you look so good to me*
> *Don't want another broken heart or a sleepless night.*
> *You're the girl of my dreams...*

Syren couldn't help but smile at the friendly gesture. If she wasn't so into Tae, she probably would've entertained the young woman, but she already had a youngster she adored. At that moment Tae came to mind, she smiled, which immediately faded after realizing she'll have some explaining to do once she made it home.

Afraid Tae would be waiting outside, she made Draco drop her off a block away from home. Her skin was sticky and sweaty plus she had a minor headache. She walked up with her hand up in an attempt to block out the blazing sun. Seeing Tae nowhere in sight outside, she knocked on the door repeatedly. Moments later, Tae opened the door, peering at Syren briefly before walking off.

"Did you call Maine to pick you up?" she asked, calmly.

Syren scowled before asking, "Wait, is my baby here?"

"No, he's at a friend's house. I dropped him off after picking them up from school."

"No, of course I didn't call Maine. He don't even know I was in jail," she admitted. "Angie picked me up," she lied.

Tae stood motionless for a moment, side-eyeing Syren. Tae didn't know the actual truth, so she had no choice but to believe her story - for now. Inwardly, she knew something wasn't right.

"What? I'm telling the truth," Syren said, putting on her best, convincing, expression.

"I didn't say nothing," Tae responded. She had no humor in her eyes. Her stare was vancat.

The longer she stared, the more uncomfortable Syren became. She made her feel like a child who just got in trouble and was awaiting punishment.

"That was some ho' shit Uh'Nija did, but she going to get hers," Tae finally spoke, breaking the silence.

She took Syren's hand into hers and led her to the bathroom, where she removed her clothing one piece at a time. Fully nude, Tae stared at Syren's body with lust-filled and hungry eyes. She led her to the tub of suds and Epsom salt. Tae stared at her eyes as she climbed into the hot water one leg at a time.

"I'll be back," she spoke softly.

Tae was so attentive. She tended to her needs with a sense of urgency. She handled her with delicacy, and Syren was loving it.

"Here, bae," Tae said as she returned with a glass of wine. She handed it to Syren, then sat on the toilet. She grabbed her leg and massaged her foot. Her stare was so intense that Syren's pussy begin to pulsate.

"I'm going to go contact this lawyer I used a few years ago in regards to your case," Tae said before leaving the restroom.

Syren had forgotten about her own case that fast.

I pray I can get out of this shit, Syren thought.

***

Two weeks later

"Call that man, Syren! I'm getting tired of him calling here. He whining and slanging snot. He say you done took everything from him. Give that boy what's his!" Shelia hollered as soon as Syren entered her home.

She hadn't seen her mother face to face since the day prior to the morning she got arrested. After reporting to the bond company, house arrest was one of her stipulations, which forced her to call those of relevance and inform them of her current situation. Maine pretended to be so surprised and upset.

After attending her court hearing, the judge granted her seven days before she began her two year sentence. Her assault charge held two to ten years. No longer out on bond, she was free to go as she pleased within the seven days. Syren had never received a parking ticket, so this was huge for her to accept.

"Momma, I'm done with Maine. I don't——"

"Who is he, Syren?" Shelia asked, peering into her eyes

"No one."

"Come on, child, who you fooling? I was born at night, but not last night."

"Momma——"

"Momma nothing, I want to know!" Sheila snapped.

"Tae," she admitted softly.

"Tae?"

"His sister, Momma."

Immediately, Shelia gasped, taken aback by her confession. "I knew it! Oooh, Syren, that's low down. You know better," Shelia voiced through squinted eyes.

"Momma, I love her——"

"When you turn gay? I didn't raise you like that."

Syren remained mute as the tears formed in her eyes.

"You know, I ain't gon' judge you. You going through enough. I'm standing by whatever you decide to do, baby girl. Do Jaelyn know?"

"Of course not. But Mom, I've made my decision. Maine was a horrible lover. Financially he was there, but being with Tae showed me what I've been missing this whole time."

Shelia nodded in response. "I just want you to go do that and come home. You know Jaelyn is in good hands," she continued, leaning in, wrapping her arms around Syren.

***

"She fucking with somebody!" Maine yelled, pacing the floor inside of the office.

"Yeah, at first I didn't believe it, but I'm starting to believe that too."

"Bruh, this bitch got two days before she goes away and you telling me she don't want no wood? Come on now, that's a freak, a big freak. That bitch not holding out. She going all out. She probably fucking three different niggas," Maine continued, venting candidly. He was heated, yet he still hadn't cut Uh'Nija off. Syren's absence was driving him.

"You got a point, man but by the same token, who would want to share dick with a cousin? She probably feel less of a woman for fucking with you after you sexed Kreesha."

"She sucked my dick!"

"Come on, Maine, I'n a nigga. It sucks to admit, but you fucked the big bitch. It's cool." He smirked, leaning back in his seat. "Big bitches need love too. I like them big. They gon' feed you, fuck you, then feed you afterwards. I like to eat."

"Fuck you, Dekari," Maine said before letting out a chuckle.

"I thought you been staking out the house?"

"I have, and I haven't seen no one but my sister leaving and coming other than Syren. Tae hates Syren, so I know she would've told me by now if some bullshit was going on. She must be doing her dirt when Tae not there."

"You know, for some reason, everything surfaces when someone either dies or get locked up. Don't stress. We'll find out sooner than later.

***

"I love you, Momma," Jaelyn expressed lacking emotion.

Syren hated that Jaelyn was so dry with her. Even after knowing she'd be away for two years, he still had no compassion in his heart. That gesture really dispirited Syren as she sat in the car preparing herself. She and Tae already had their goodbye talk before and a long night of hot steaming sex, which wasn't enough for Tae. She begged Syren for the opportunity to at least walk her inside so they'd have a few more seconds alone.

"I love you, baby girl. Chin up, chest out. Go ahead and get it over with. We waiting on you," Sheila announced while the tears streamed down her face. Her puffy eyes were proof she'd been crying for days.

"Quit crying, Momma, I love you too," Syren said, stepping out of the car.

Shelia did so well and they embraced for what felt like hours.

"Awww, Syren, baby, just know real bitches do real shit. I got you, girl," Angie said, wrapping her arms around her dispirited friend.

Syren hugged her back with the little strength she had left.

"Okay, okay, this is it, y'all," she said, peering at the four of them.

"Come on, Tae," she mumbled while waving and blowing kisses at the others.

As soon as Syren turned to walk away, she cried even harder.

"I hope this isn't my last time seeing you," she spoke softly through sniffles, walking slowly inside the county jail

"Why would you say something like that?" Tae asked looking into her eyes.

"I don't know. I just feel that way," she spoke.

"I promise you I'm not going anywhere. I'm gon' hold you down to the fullest. I don't give a damn what happens. I love you. You got my soul. We not just lovers. We family," she expressed, then kissed Syren in the center of her forehead.

***

Dekari had told Maine to be camping out on this very day, but he didn't bring up the fact that he overslept from partying all night at the club with Uh'Nija ho' ass. Although Maine couldn't make it, Dekari could, and he couldn't wait to break the unbelievable news to his friend. The funny part was, Dekari wasn't the only one staked outfront. Draco was there as well.

Chapter 15
Everything out in the open

Three weeks had passed, and so far Tae had kept her promise. She visited Syren once a week and kept funds on her phone and commissary. She even sent a galore of pictures. The first two visits she brought Jaelyn and Shelia along. Today, she visited alone. Syren had just finished wiping her cum on the glass when the C.O. announced, "Times up." She promised Tae a show the next visit and a show is what she got.

"I love you, bae!" Syren called out, being led away by the C.O.

"I love you too," Tae shot back with a huge grin, showcasing her deep dimples. Tae watched Syren until she was no longer in her view. She turned around, bumping into a guy by accident.

"My bad."

The presence of Maine ceased Tae's speech.

"So you bae? Really, bruh? You know, Dekari tried to tell me, and I didn't listen. You my family, dawg. We've slept in the same bed, shared clothes, and you go fuck the bitch I was about to make my wife?" Maine inquired through squinted eyes and clenched teeth. Maine looked deranged.

"I do apologize for allowing it to happen, but it did. This is what it is. Team Us."

Maine tucked his lips underneath and placed his hand on his hip while peering around slowly. "You lucky you're my mother's child and losing you will break her heart, 'cause I'll kill you, bitch."

Tae peered into his eyes, unfazed by the threat.

"Come on, Maine, you know it's nothing pussy about me but the split between my legs. Don't threaten me. Just know when you come for me, be prepared to die too. That blood shit ain't gon' make me let up. I ain't scared of you, boy. I already apologized. Whatever you want to do, we can do it," Tae stated, throwing up her hands.

"Yeah, that gangsta shit, it sounds good."

***

"This is No Limit Bails Bond. Are you a close relative of a Syren Wiley?"

"Yes I am, how may I help you?" Tae announced, wiping the sleep from her eyes.

"I'm trying to get a Dra'Neisha Collins, who cosigned on her bond."

"Dra'Neisha?" Tae repeated.

"Yes, Dra'Neisha Collins. She put an $1,800 tennis bracelet up for collateral and we're trying to contact her to see if she has the payment for the asset. If she doesn't appear in 48 hours we will keep it as a form of payment and she won't be able to get it back."

"Okay. Thanks."

Tae smiled, shaking her head while peering straight ahead in pure disbelief. One thing she hated was a liar. She'd given Syren everything just to get slapped in the face in return. Her hands began to tremble. She was so upset.

***

Maine walked inside the jail. He was ready to face Syren. After undergoing the proper procedure, he sat on the steel, awaiting Syren's arrival. He was as jittery as a coke head who just snorted too many lines.

Syren entered the booth with a huge grin that quickly faded after spotting Maine. She was hoping it was Tae. "What do you want, Maine?" she asked, rolling her eyes without taking a seat.

"You know, Syren, for the longest, I was looking for Terry, Michael, and Del when all the time it was Bre'untae that was sleeping with my girl. Aunty Tae want to be stepdad, huh?"

"You're crazy and I'm leaving," Syren stated.

"Hold on. I'm pretty sure you already know about the run-in Tae and I had? I just want you to know this," he said, standing to his feet. "My son won't be around that homo shit. I'm filing for full custody."

"For what? Bitch, your heart is black as your skin. I hate you! All I did was do you how you did me and fuck your relative!" Syren yelled at Maine's back. "You can't take my son from me!" she shouted as the C.O.'s dragged her out.

All that night, Syren had been crying her eyes out. Hurt was only half of it. Her heart ached and she felt soulless on top of it all. Tae hadn't answered her mail or calls. Something told her Tae was in some sort of trouble. Maine, on the other hand, was beyond upset. She had never saw him so demonic. The dispassionate and stoic look in his eyes sent chills up her spine.

***

"Iesha Jenkins, you have mail," the C.O. announced as she sat at the steel table in her cell.

Iesha headed downstairs. She had been locked up for quite some time now. She pretty much ran shit. The C.O.'s referred to her as the "dorm boss". She only had two fights her entire incarceration, but she was well respected. She could hear her father's words in her ear. "Everywhere you go, you have to set the atmosphere. Some will get in the way while doing so, and that's when you make a good example. The rest will fall back."

"What's your number?"

"3046712."

The C.O. handed Iesha a jpay and an envelope, both from Tae.

Iesha quickly returned to her cell. Mack and Iesha were together. Mack knew all about Tae. Mack knew her and Iesha's relationship ended as soon either of them were released.

"That must be that nigga got you smiling that hard."

"Don't start," she said, rolling her eyes.

The longer they dated, the more jealous Mack had become. In Iesha's eyes, Mack was just something to do. She wasn't the first, and surely not the last. She loved Tae's dirty drawers and even though she didn't do any of it out of spite, fucking with chicks was just an easier way to do her time.

***

"Wiley, mail call."

Syren wiped her eyes and rushed downstairs, hoping it was from Tae. She flashed her ID to the C.O. and collected her mail. A huge grin formed once she spotted Tae's name on the mail, but she scowled at the length prior to reading it.

Syren,

Honestly I haven't been feeling you since I found out you looked me into my eyes and lied I want to be the first to tell you that me and Iesha are going strong. She was released yesterday due to the COVID-19 breakout. Peace

Syren unconsciously dropped the single sheet of paper. She grabbed her chest to calm her heartbeat. She peered around quickly as her breathing became shallow.

"I can't do this," she whispered, peering around the dorm. She took deep breaths, gagging in the process. Tears were now streaming down her face. She was in a state of shock.

"No, no, no, no, no, this can't be true," Syren whispered, rocking back and forth staring ahead blankly. Seconds later, everything went black.

*****

"Hey baby, look, you have to be strong. You losing weight. I can see it in your face," she preached from the other side of the grass.

"I know, Momma, but I've lost Tae and Maine hates me too. I don't have shit."

"You got me and Jaelyn. Speaking of Jaelyn, Maine up here today doing the paperwork to attain custody."

Together, Sheila and Syren shook their heads.
***

On the other side of town, Maine stood eyeing the guy who had swabbed his mouth a few days ago to get his DNA. He blew out a frustrated sigh at the ridiculous procedure. He felt as if this part of the procedure didn't pertain to him.

"Mr. Wiley——"

"Yes? Can I have my results so we can get to the next part?" Maine requested rudely.

The guy blinked a few times before responding. "Mr. Wiley, according to the test results, you are 99.9% not Jaelyn Wiley's father. Therefore, you will not…"

Every word after "not" was unheard. The tears burned his eye sockets instantly and he felt his cheeks and toes heat up.

Jittery, he stood there, staring blankly ahead. The news was unexpected.

***

Syren had been awake all night. She knew that the truth had surfaced by now. Everything was out in the open, and there was nothing left to hide. Her past had come to haunt her. CPS had gotten involved after assuming she was an unfit parent - due to her incarceration, that is. Maine even went to the extent of making false complaints on Shelia to make it an easy win, not knowing he was never in the race. According to Sheila, he admitted feeling bad for lying on her parenting skills, but now they were on the verge of losing Jaelyn.

Syren tottered over to the pay phone and called her mother. Her heart was racing as it rang. Since talking on the phone, it had brought nothing but pain and heartache.

"Hello?" Syren mumbled.

"Syren. These folks just left. They trying to take Jaelyn. I'm not standing for it. I know you don't want to hurt that man's feelings, but the damage is done. You're either going to tell him, or I am. His father has to go obtain custody before the state takes full custody of my baby!"

"Yes ma'am, tell him to come see me."

Click!

Syren took a deep breath and awaited her visit. She had to tell him the truth.

If you thought that I was perfect,
Boy, you were wrong. I'm far from that
There's one thing that I've done to you
That I regret and I know there's
No excuse, but I'm only human and

Young at that, see I'm going to make
Mistakes. I hope you understand.
Didn't see it coming, wasn't on purpose
Baby, I promise I didn't mean to hurt you,
I promise I didn't mean to hurt you.
Do you forgive me? 'Cause I know it
Wasn't worth it. Gotta tell em the truth...

***

The next day, Syren was awakened by the C.O. shouting her name. After pondering all night, she refused to look into his eyes and confess the disheartening news.

"Syren Wiley!"

Syren rushed downstairs, running directly into the C.O., Mr. Tibbs.

"Mr. Tibbs, I'm refusing my visit, but can you please give him this?" Syren asked, handing him the torn sheet of paper.

"Why?"

"Long story," she responded, lowering her head.

"Okay, I got you, Wiley," he agreed, leaving the dorm.

***

Maine sat on the steel bed with his face buried into the palms of his hands. All his wrongs had come back to bite him in the ass. All the hoes, the threesomes, one night stands, and all the lies and scandals. And on top of it all, it wasn't over. He waited for Syren to break him the last bit of heart-wrenching news when an older C.O. walked in, opening the door behind him. Maine scowled, confused by his presence rather than Syren's.

193

"Sir, Ms. Wiley will not be attending her visit. She refused, but she told me to give you this."

Maine's hand shook uncontrollably as he unfolded the small sheet of paper that read:

"Tell Dekari to go get my son."

To Be Continued...
Levels to This Shyt 2
Coming Soon

Submission Guideline

Submit the first three chapters of your completed manuscript to ldpsubmissions@gmail.com, subject line: Your book's title. The manuscript must be in a .doc file and sent as an attachment. Document should be in Times New Roman, double spaced and in size 12 font. Also, provide your synopsis and full contact information. If sending multiple submissions, they must each be in a separate email.

Have a story but no way to send it electronically? You can still submit to LDP/Ca$h Presents. Send in the first three chapters, written or typed, of your completed manuscript to:

LDP: Submissions Dept
Po Box 944
Stockbridge, Ga 30281

DO NOT send original manuscript. Must be a duplicate.

Provide your synopsis and a cover letter containing your full contact information.

Thanks for considering LDP and Ca$h Presents.

<u>Coming Soon from Lock Down Publications/Ca$h Presents</u>

BOW DOWN TO MY GANGSTA
By **Ca$h**
TORN BETWEEN TWO
By **Coffee**
THE STREETS STAINED MY SOUL **II**
By **Marcellus Allen**
BLOOD OF A BOSS **VI**
SHADOWS OF THE GAME II
By **Askari**
LOYAL TO THE GAME **IV**
By **T.J. & Jelissa**
IF LOVING YOU IS WRONG… **III**
By **Jelissa**
TRUE SAVAGE **VIII**
MIDNIGHT CARTEL III
DOPE BOY MAGIC IV
CITY OF KINGZ II
By **Chris Green**
BLAST FOR ME **III**
A SAVAGE DOPEBOY III
CUTTHROAT MAFIA III
DUFFLE BAG CARTEL VI
By **Ghost**
A HUSTLER'S DECEIT III
KILL ZONE **II**

BAE BELONGS TO ME III

A DOPE BOY'S QUEEN III

By **Aryanna**

COKE KINGS V

KING OF THE TRAP II

By **T.J. Edwards**

GORILLAZ IN THE BAY V

3X KRAZY II

De'Kari

THE STREETS ARE CALLING II

Duquie Wilson

KINGPIN KILLAZ IV

STREET KINGS III

PAID IN BLOOD III

CARTEL KILLAZ IV

DOPE GODS III

Hood Rich

SINS OF A HUSTLA II

ASAD

KINGZ OF THE GAME VI

Playa Ray

SLAUGHTER GANG IV

RUTHLESS HEART IV

By Willie Slaughter

THE HEART OF A SAVAGE III

By Jibril Williams

FUK SHYT II

By Blakk Diamond

TRAP QUEEN

By Troublesome

YAYO V

GHOST MOB II

Stilloan Robinson

KINGPIN DREAMS III

By Paper Boi Rari

CREAM II

By Yolanda Moore

SON OF A DOPE FIEND III

By Renta

FOREVER GANGSTA II

GLOCKS ON SATIN SHEETS III

By Adrian Dulan

LOYALTY AIN'T PROMISED III

By Keith Williams

THE PRICE YOU PAY FOR LOVE II

By Destiny Skai

CONFESSIONS OF A GANGSTA III

By Nicholas Lock

I'M NOTHING WITHOUT HIS LOVE II

SINS OF A THUG II

By Monet Dragun

LIFE OF A SAVAGE IV

MURDA SEASON IV

GANGLAND CARTEL III

CHI'RAQ GANGSTAS II

By **Romell Tukes**

QUIET MONEY IV

THUG LIFE II

EXTENDED CLIP II

By **Trai'Quan**

THE STREETS MADE ME III

By **Larry D. Wright**

IF YOU CROSS ME ONCE II

ANGEL III

By **Anthony Fields**

FRIEND OR FOE III

By **Mimi**

SAVAGE STORMS II

By **Meesha**

BLOOD ON THE MONEY III

By J-Blunt

THE STREETS WILL NEVER CLOSE II

By K'ajji

NIGHTMARES OF A HUSTLA III

By King Dream

THE WIFEY I USED TO BE II

By Nicole Goosby

IN THE ARM OF HIS BOSS

By Jamila

MONEY, MURDER & MEMORIES II

Malik D. Rice

CONCRETE KILLAZ II

By Kingpen

HARD AND RUTHLESS II

By Von Wiley Hall

LEVELS TO THIS SHYT II

By Ah'Million

Available Now

RESTRAINING ORDER **I & II**

By **CA$H & Coffee**

LOVE KNOWS NO BOUNDARIES **I II & III**

By **Coffee**

RAISED AS A GOON I, II, III & IV

BRED BY THE SLUMS I, II, III

BLAST FOR ME I & II

ROTTEN TO THE CORE I II III

A BRONX TALE I, II, III

DUFFLE BAG CARTEL I II III IV V

HEARTLESS GOON I II III IV

A SAVAGE DOPEBOY I II

HEARTLESS GOON I II III

DRUG LORDS I II III

CUTTHROAT MAFIA I II

By **Ghost**

LAY IT DOWN **I & II**

LAST OF A DYING BREED I II

Levels to This Shyt

BLOOD STAINS OF A SHOTTA I & II III

By **Jamaica**

LOYAL TO THE GAME I II III

LIFE OF SIN I, II III

By **TJ & Jelissa**

BLOODY COMMAS I & II

SKI MASK CARTEL I II & III

KING OF NEW YORK I II,III IV V

RISE TO POWER I II III

COKE KINGS I II III IV

BORN HEARTLESS I II III IV

KING OF THE TRAP

By **T.J. Edwards**

IF LOVING HIM IS WRONG…I & II

LOVE ME EVEN WHEN IT HURTS I II III

By **Jelissa**

WHEN THE STREETS CLAP BACK I & II III

THE HEART OF A SAVAGE I II

By **Jibril Williams**

A DISTINGUISHED THUG STOLE MY HEART I II & III

LOVE SHOULDN'T HURT I II III IV

RENEGADE BOYS I II III IV

PAID IN KARMA I II III

SAVAGE STORMS

By **Meesha**

A GANGSTER'S CODE I &, II III

A GANGSTER'S SYN I II III

Ah'Million

THE SAVAGE LIFE I II III
CHAINED TO THE STREETS I II III
BLOOD ON THE MONEY I II
By J-Blunt
PUSH IT TO THE LIMIT
By **Bre' Hayes**
BLOOD OF A BOSS **I, II, III, IV, V**
SHADOWS OF THE GAME
By **Askari**
THE STREETS BLEED MURDER **I, II & III**
THE HEART OF A GANGSTA I II& III
By **Jerry Jackson**
CUM FOR ME I II III IV V VI
An **LDP Erotica Collaboration**
BRIDE OF A HUSTLA **I II & II**
THE FETTI GIRLS **I, II& III**
CORRUPTED BY A GANGSTA I, II III, IV
BLINDED BY HIS LOVE
THE PRICE YOU PAY FOR LOVE
DOPE GIRL MAGIC I II III
By **Destiny Skai**
WHEN A GOOD GIRL GOES BAD
By **Adrienne**
THE COST OF LOYALTY I II III
By Kweli
A GANGSTER'S REVENGE **I II III & IV**
THE BOSS MAN'S DAUGHTERS I II III IV V

202

A SAVAGE LOVE **I & II**

BAE BELONGS TO ME I II

A HUSTLER'S DECEIT I, II, III

WHAT BAD BITCHES DO I, II, III

SOUL OF A MONSTER I II III

KILL ZONE

A DOPE BOY'S QUEEN I II

By **Aryanna**

A KINGPIN'S AMBITON

A KINGPIN'S AMBITION **II**

I MURDER FOR THE DOUGH

By **Ambitious**

TRUE SAVAGE I II III IV V VI VII

DOPE BOY MAGIC I, II, III

MIDNIGHT CARTEL I II

CITY OF KINGZ

By **Chris Green**

A DOPEBOY'S PRAYER

By **Eddie "Wolf" Lee**

THE KING CARTEL **I, II & III**

By **Frank Gresham**

THESE NIGGAS AIN'T LOYAL **I, II & III**

By **Nikki Tee**

GANGSTA SHYT **I II &III**

By **CATO**

THE ULTIMATE BETRAYAL

By **Phoenix**

Ah'Million

BOSS'N UP **I , II & III**
By **Royal Nicole**
I LOVE YOU TO DEATH
By Destiny J
I RIDE FOR MY HITTA
I STILL RIDE FOR MY HITTA
By **Misty Holt**
LOVE & CHASIN' PAPER
By **Qay Crockett**
TO DIE IN VAIN
SINS OF A HUSTLA
By **ASAD**
BROOKLYN HUSTLAZ
By **Boogsy Morina**
BROOKLYN ON LOCK I & II
By **Sonovia**
GANGSTA CITY
By **Teddy Duke**
A DRUG KING AND HIS DIAMOND I & II III
A DOPEMAN'S RICHES
HER MAN, MINE'S TOO I, II
CASH MONEY HO'S
THE WIFEY I USED TO BE
By Nicole Goosby
TRAPHOUSE KING **I II & III**
KINGPIN KILLAZ I II III
STREET KINGS I II

204

Levels to This Shyt

PAID IN BLOOD **I II**

CARTEL KILLAZ I II III

DOPE GODS I II

By **Hood Rich**

LIPSTICK KILLAH **I, II, III**

CRIME OF PASSION I II & III

FRIEND OR FOE I II

By **Mimi**

STEADY MOBBN' **I, II, III**

THE STREETS STAINED MY SOUL

By **Marcellus Allen**

WHO SHOT YA **I, II, III**

SON OF A DOPE FIEND I II

Renta

GORILLAZ IN THE BAY **I II III IV**

TEARS OF A GANGSTA I II

3X KRAZY

DE'KARI

TRIGGADALE I II III

Elijah R. Freeman

GOD BLESS THE TRAPPERS I, II, III

THESE SCANDALOUS STREETS I, II, III

FEAR MY GANGSTA I, II, III IV, V

THESE STREETS DON'T LOVE NOBODY I, II

BURY ME A G I, II, III, IV, V

A GANGSTA'S EMPIRE I, II, III, IV

THE DOPEMAN'S BODYGAURD I II

THE REALEST KILLAZ I II III

Tranay Adams

THE STREETS ARE CALLING

Duquie Wilson

MARRIED TO A BOSS... I II III

By Destiny Skai & Chris Green

KINGZ OF THE GAME I II III IV V

Playa Ray

SLAUGHTER GANG I II III

RUTHLESS HEART I II III

By Willie Slaughter

FUK SHYT

By Blakk Diamond

DON'T F#CK WITH MY HEART I II

By Linnea

ADDICTED TO THE DRAMA I II III

IN THE ARM OF HIS BOSS II

By Jamila

YAYO I II III IV

A SHOOTER'S AMBITION I II

By S. Allen

TRAP GOD I II III

By Troublesome

FOREVER GANGSTA

GLOCKS ON SATIN SHEETS I II

By Adrian Dulan

TOE TAGZ I II III

LEVELS TO THIS SHYT

By Ah'Million

KINGPIN DREAMS I II

By Paper Boi Rari

CONFESSIONS OF A GANGSTA I II

By Nicholas Lock

I'M NOTHING WITHOUT HIS LOVE

SINS OF A THUG

By Monet Dragun

CAUGHT UP IN THE LIFE I II III

By Robert Baptiste

NEW TO MONEY, MURDER & MEMORIES

THE GAME I II III

By **Malik D. Rice**

LIFE OF A SAVAGE I II III

A GANGSTA'S QUR'AN I II III

MURDA SEASON I II III

GANGLAND CARTEL I II

CHI'RAQ GANGSTAS

By **Romell Tukes**

LOYALTY AIN'T PROMISED I II

By Keith Williams

QUIET MONEY I II III

THUG LIFE

EXTENDED CLIP

By **Trai'Quan**

THE STREETS MADE ME I II

Ah'Million

By **Larry D. Wright**
THE ULTIMATE SACRIFICE I, II, III, IV, V, VI
KHADIFI
IF YOU CROSS ME ONCE
ANGEL I II
By **Anthony Fields**
THE LIFE OF A HOOD STAR
By **Ca$h & Rashia Wilson**
THE STREETS WILL NEVER CLOSE
By **K'ajji**
CREAM
By **Yolanda Moore**
NIGHTMARES OF A HUSTLA I II
By **King Dream**
CONCRETE KILLAZ
By **Kingpen**
HARD AND RUTHLESS
By **Von Wiley Hall**
GHOST MOB II
Stilloan Robinson

BOOKS BY LDP'S CEO, CA$H

TRUST IN NO MAN

TRUST IN NO MAN 2

TRUST IN NO MAN 3

BONDED BY BLOOD

SHORTY GOT A THUG

THUGS CRY

THUGS CRY 2

THUGS CRY 3

TRUST NO BITCH

TRUST NO BITCH 2

TRUST NO BITCH 3

TIL MY CASKET DROPS

RESTRAINING ORDER

RESTRAINING ORDER 2

IN LOVE WITH A CONVICT

LIFE OF A HOOD STAR

Ah'Million